Holly Goldberg Sloan

counting
by 7s

dial books for young readers

an imprint of Penguin Group (USA) inc.

Dial Books for Young Readers
Published by the Penguin Group
Penguin Group (USA) Inc., 375 Hudson Street,
New York, New York 10014, USA

USA / Canada / UK / Ireland / Australia / New Zealand / India / South Africa / China
Penguin Books Ltd, Registered Offices: 80 Strand, London WC2R 0RL, England
For more information about the Penguin Group visit penguin.com

Sloan, Holly Goldberg, date.
Counting by 7s / Holly Goldberg Sloan.
p. cm.
Summary: Twelve-year-old genius and outsider Willow Chance must figure out how to connect
with other people and find a surrogate family for herself after her parents are killed in a car accident.
ISBN 978-0-8037-3855-3 (hardcover)
[1. Genius—Fiction. 2. Eccentrics and eccentricities—Fiction. 3. High schools—Fiction. 4. Schools—Fiction.
5. Orphans—Fiction. 6. Gardening—Fiction.] I. Title. II. Title: Counting by sevens.
PZ7.S633136Cou 2012   [Fic]—dc23   2012004994

Printed in the United States of America
13 15 17 19 20 18 16 14

Book design by Mina Chung

For Chuck Sloan
&
Lisa Gaiser Urick
2 of the 7 . . .

chapter 1

willow chance

*A genius shoots at something no
one else can see, and hits it.*

⟨◦∿◦⟩

We sit together outside the Fosters Freeze at a
sea-green, metal picnic table.

All four of us.

We eat soft ice cream, which has been plunged into a
vat of liquid chocolate (that then hardens into a crispy
shell).

I don't tell anyone that what makes this work is wax.
Or to be more accurate: edible, food-grade paraffin wax.

As the chocolate cools, it holds the vanilla goodness
prisoner.

Our job is to set it free.

Ordinarily, I don't even eat ice-cream cones. And if I
do, I obsess in such a precise way as to prevent even a
drop of disorder.

But not today.

I'm in a public place.

I'm not even spying.

And my ice-cream cone is a big, drippy mess.

I'm right now someone that other people might find interesting to observe.

Why?

Well first of all, I'm speaking Vietnamese, which is not my "native tongue."

I really like that expression because in general, I think people don't give this contracting muscle credit for how much work it does.

So thank you, tongue.

Sitting here, shaded by the afternoon sun, I'm using my Vietnamese whenever I can, which turns out to be often.

I'm talking to my new friend Mai, but even her always-surly and scary-because-he's-older big brother, Quang-ha, says a few words to me in their now only semi-secret language.

Dell Duke, who brought us here in his car, is quiet.

He does not speak Vietnamese.

I do not like to exclude people (I'm the one who is always excluded, so I know how *that* feels), but I'm okay with Mr. Duke being an observer. He is a school counselor and listening is a big part of counseling.

Or at least it should be.

Mai does the lion's share of the speaking and eating (I give her my cone once I've had enough), and all I know for certain, with the sun on our faces and the sweet ice cream holding our attention, is that this is a day that I will never forget.

Seventeen minutes after our arrival, we are back in Dell Duke's car.

Mai wants to drive by Hagen Oaks, which is a park. Big geese live there year-round. She thinks I should see them.

Because she's two years older than me, she falls into that trap of thinking all little kids want to stare at something like fat ducks.

Don't get me wrong. I appreciate waterfowl.

But in the case of Hagen Oaks Park, I'm more interested in the city's decision to plant native plants than I am in the birds.

I think by the look on Dell's face (I can see his eyes in the rearview mirror) that he's not very excited about either thing, but he drives by the park anyway.

Quang-ha is slumped in the seat and I'm guessing is just happy that he didn't have to take a bus anywhere.

At Hagen Oaks, no one gets out of the car, because Dell says we need to go home.

When we first got to the Fosters Freeze, I called my mom to explain that I'd be late getting back from school. When she didn't answer, I left a message.

I did the same thing on my dad's cell phone.

It's strange that I haven't heard from either of them.

If they can't answer the phone, they always quickly return my call.

Always.

There is a police car parked in the driveway of my house when Dell Duke turns onto my street.

The neighbors to the south of us moved out and their place is in foreclosure. A sign on the dead front lawn says BANK OWNED.

To the north are renters who I have only seen once 7 months and four days ago, which was on the day that they arrived.

I stare at the police car and wonder if someone broke into the vacant house.

Didn't Mom say it was trouble to have an empty place in the neighborhood?

But that wouldn't explain why the police are in *our* driveway.

As we get closer I can see that there are two officers in the patrol car. And from the way they are slouched, it seems like they've been there a while.

I feel my whole body tense.

In the front seat, Quang-ha says:

"What are the cops doing in your driveway?"

Mai's eyes dart from her brother back to me. The expression on her face now looks to be a question.

I think she wonders if my dad steals things, or if I have a cousin who hits people. Maybe I come from a whole family of troublemakers?

We don't know each other very well, so these would all be possibilities.

I'm silent.

I'm late coming home. Did my mom or my dad get so worried that they called the police?

I left them messages.

I told them that I was okay.

I can't believe that they would do such a thing.

Dell Duke doesn't even have the car completely stopped before I open the door, which is of course dangerous.

I get out and head toward my house, not even bothering with my red rolling luggage that's packed with my schoolwork.

I've taken only two steps into the driveway before the door opens on the patrol car and a female officer appears.

The woman has a thick ponytail of orange-colored hair.

She doesn't say hello. She just lowers her sunglasses and says:

"Do you know Roberta and James Chance?"

I try to answer, but my voice won't come out any louder than a whisper:

"Yes."

I want to add: "But it's Jimmy Chance. No one calls my dad James."

But I can't.

The officer fumbles with her sunglasses. Even though she is dressed the part, the woman seems to be losing all of her authority.

She mumbles:

"Okay . . . And you are . . . ?"

I swallow, but my mouth is suddenly dry and I feel a lump form in my throat.

"I'm their daughter . . ."

Dell Duke is out of the car now and he has my luggage with him as he starts across the sidewalk. Mai is right at his heels. Quang-ha stays put.

The second officer, a younger man, then comes around and stands next to his partner. But neither of them speaks.

Just silence.

Horrible silence.

And then the two police officers turn their attention to

Dell. They both look anxious. The female officer manages to say:

"And where do you fit in . . . ?"

Dell clears his throat. He suddenly looks like he's sweating from every gland in his body. He is barely able to speak:

"I'm Dell D-D-Duke. I work as a c-c-counselor for the school district. I see two of these k-k-kids for counseling. I'm just d-d-driving them home."

I can see that both officers are instantly relieved.

The female officer begins nodding, showing support and almost enthusiasm as she says:

"A counselor? So she heard?"

I find enough of a voice to ask:

"Heard what?"

But neither of the police will look at me. They are all about Dell now.

"Can we have a word with you, sir?"

I watch Dell's sweaty wet hand release from the black vinyl luggage handle, and he follows the officers as they move away from me, away from the patrol car, and out to the still-hot pavement of the street.

Standing there, they huddle together with their backs turned so that as I watch, they look, lit by the low, end-of-the-day sun, like an evil, three-headed monster.

And that's what they are because their voices, while muffled, are still capable of being understood.

I clearly hear four words:

"There's been an accident."

And after that in whispers comes the news that the two people I love most in the world are gone forever.

No.

No.

No.

No.

No.

No.

No.

I need to rewind.

I want to go back.

Will anyone go with me?

chapter 2

two months ago

❧

I'm about to start a new school.

I'm an only child.

I'm adopted.

And I'm different.

As in strange.

But I know it and that takes the edge off. At least for
me.

Is it possible to be loved too much?

My

Two

Parents

Really

Truly

L-O-V-E

Me.

I think waiting a long time for something makes it more
gratifying.

The correlation between expectation and delivery of desire could no doubt be quantified into some kind of mathematical formula.

But that's off the point, which is one of my problems and why despite the fact that I'm a thinker, I'm never the teacher's pet.

Ever.

Right now I'm going to stick to the facts.

For 7 years my mom tried to get pregnant.

That seems like a long time of working at something, since the medical definition of infertility is twelve months of well-timed physical union without any results.

And while I have a passion for all things medical, the idea of them doing that, especially with any kind of regularity and enthusiasm, makes me feel nauseated (as medically defined, an unpleasant sensation in the abdomen).

Twice in those years my mom peed on a plastic wand, and turned the diagnostic instrument blue.

But twice she couldn't keep the fetus. (How onomatopoetic is that word? *Fetus.* Insane.)

Her cake failed to bake.

And that's how I came into the mix.

On the 7th day of the 7th month (is it any wonder I love the number?) my new parents drove north to a hospital 257 miles from their home, where they named me after a cold-climate tree and changed the world.

Or at least our world.

Time out. It probably wasn't 257 miles, but that's how I need to think of it. (2 + 5 = 7. And 257 is a prime number. Super-special. There is order in my universe.)

Back to adoption day. As my dad explains it, I never once cried, but my mom did all the way down Interstate Five South until exit 17B.

My mom weeps when she's happy. When she's sad, she's just quiet.

I believe that her emotional wiring got crossed in this area. We deal with it because most of the time she's smiling. Very wide.

When my two new parents finally made it to our single-story, stucco house in a development at the end of the San Joaquin Valley, their nerves were both shot.

And our family adventure had just begun.

I think it's important to get pictures of things in your head. Even if they are wrong. And they pretty much always are.

If you could see me, you would say that I don't fit into an easily identifiable ethnic category.

I'm what's called "a person of color."

And my parents are not.

They are two of the whitest white people in the world (no exaggeration).

They are so white, they are almost blue. They don't have circulation problems; they just don't have much pigment.

My mom has fine, red hair and eyes that are pale, pale, pale blue. So pale they look gray. Which they are not.

My dad is tall and pretty much bald. He has seborrheic dermatitis, which means that his skin appears to be constantly in a state of rash.

This has led to a great deal of observation and research on my part, but for him it is no picnic.

If you are now picturing this trio and considering us together, I want you to know that while I don't in any way resemble my parents, somehow we just naturally look like a family.

At least I think so.

And that's all that really matters.

Besides the number 7, I have two other major obsessions. Medical conditions. And plants.

By medical conditions, I mean human disease.

I study myself, of course. But *my* illnesses have been minor and not life-threatening.

I do observe and chronicle my mom and dad, but they will not let me do much diagnostic work on their behalf.

The only reason that I regularly leave the house (not counting going to the forced-prison-camp also known as middle school and my weekly trip to the central library) is to observe sickness in the general population.

It would always be my first choice to sit for several hours every day in a hospital, but it turns out that nursing staffs have a problem with that.

Even if you're just camped out in a waiting room pretending to read a book.

So I visit the local shopping mall, which fortunately has its share of disease.

But I don't buy things.

Since I was little, I've kept field notes and made diagnostic flash cards.

I am particularly drawn to skin disorders, which I photograph only if the subject (and one of my parents) isn't looking.

My second interest: plants.

They are living, growing, reproducing, pushing and pulling in the ground all around us at all times.

We accept that without even noticing.

Open your eyes, people.

This is amazing.

If plants made sounds, it would all be different. But they communicate with color and shape and size and texture.

They don't meow or bark or tweet.

We think they don't have eyes, but they see the angle of the sun and the rise of the moon. They don't just *feel* the wind; they change directions because of it.

Before you think I'm crazy (which is always a possibility), look outside.

Right now.

I'm hoping that your view isn't of a parking lot or the side of a building.

I'm imagining you see a tall tree with delicate leaves. You catch sight of swaying grass in a wide field. Weeds pushing up through a crack in the sidewalk are in the distance somewhere. We are surrounded.

I'm asking you to pay attention in a new way and view it all as being Alive.

With a capital *A*.

My hometown, like a lot of the central valley of California, has a desert climate and is flat and dry and very hot for over half of the year.

Since I've never lived anywhere else, whole months of days where it's 100 degrees outside seems normal.

We call it summer.

Despite the heat, there is no escaping the fact that the bright sun and rich soil make the area ideal for growing things once you add water to the equation.

And I did.

So where once our house had a rectangle of grass, there is now a forty-foot-high stand of timber bamboo.

I have citrus trees (orange, grapefruit, and lime) next to my year-round vegetable garden.

I grow grapes, a variety of vines, annual and perennial flowers, and, in one small area, tropical plants.

To know me is to know my garden.

It is my sanctuary.

It's sort of tragic that we can't remember the earliest of the early years.

I feel as if these memories could be the key to the whole "Who am I?" question.

What was my first nightmare about?

How did the first step really feel?

What was the decision-making process when it came time to ditch the diapers?

I've got some toddler memories, but my first sequence recall is kindergarten; no matter how hard I've tried to forget the experience.

My parents said the place was going to be all kinds of fun.

It wasn't.

The school was only blocks from our house, and it was here that I first committed the crime of questioning the system.

The instructor, Mrs. King, had just plowed her way through a popular picture book. It featured the hallmarks of most pre-school literature: repetition, some kind of annoying rhyming, and bold-faced scientific lies.

I remember Mrs. King asking the class:

"How does this book make you feel?"

The appropriate answer, as far as she was concerned, was "tired," because the overly cheery instructor forced us to lie down on sticky rubber mats for twenty minutes after "lunchtime picture book."

Half of the class usually fell deeply asleep.

I remember distinctly a boy named Miles twice peeing his pants, and, with the exception of a kid named Garrison (who I'm certain had some sort of restless leg syndrome), everyone else in the room seemed to actually enjoy the horizontal break.

What were these kids thinking?

That first week while my classmates dozed off, I obsessively worried about the hygiene of the linoleum floor.

I can still hear Mrs. King, spine straight and shrill voice booming:

"How does this book make you *feel?*"

She then made a few exaggerated yawns.

I recall looking around at my fellow inmates, thinking: *Would someone, anyone, just shout out the word* tired?

I had not uttered a single syllable in my five sessions as a student, and I had no intention of doing so.

But after days of hearing more lies from an adult than I'd been exposed to in my whole lifetime—everything from how fairies cleaned up the classroom at night to insane explanations for earthquake preparedness kits—I was at some kind of breaking point.

So when the teacher specifically said:

"Willow, how does this book make *you* feel?"

I had to tell the truth:

"It makes me feel really bad. The moon can't hear someone say good night; it is two hundred thirty-five thousand miles away. And bunnies don't live in houses. Also, I don't think that the artwork is very interesting."

I bit my lower lip and experienced the metallic taste of blood.

"But really, hearing you read the book makes me feel bad mostly because I know it means you are going to make us lie down on the floor—and germs there could make us sick. There's a thing called salmonella and it is very dangerous. Especially to kids."

That afternoon, I learned the word *weirdo* because that's what I was called by the other kids.

When my mom came to pick me up, she found me crying behind the Dumpster in the play yard.

I was taken to see an educational consultant that autumn and the woman did an evaluation. She sent my parents a letter.

I read it.

It said I was "highly gifted."

Are people "lowly gifted"?

Or "medium gifted"?

Or just "gifted"? It's possible that all labels are curses. Unless they are on cleaning products.

Because in my opinion it's not really a great idea to see people as one thing.

Every person has lots of ingredients to make them into what is always a one-of-a-kind creation.

We are all imperfect genetic stews.

According to the consultant, Mrs. Grace V. Mirman,

the challenge for the parents of someone "highly gifted" was to find ways to keep the child engaged and stimulated.

But I think she was wrong.

Almost everything interests me.

I can be engaged by the arc of the water in a sprinkler system. I can look through a microscope for a shockingly long period of time.

The challenge for my parents was going to be to find friends who could put up with such a person.

All of this leads to our garden.

Mom and Dad said that they were looking to enrich my life. But I think one thing was obvious from the beginning:

Plants can't talk back.

chapter 3

❧

As a family, we threw ourselves into growing things. I have photos from the early trips to buy seeds and pick out young plants. I look insanely excited.

Early on, I adopted my gardening outfit.

It did not change over the years.

You could say it was my uniform.

I almost always wore a khaki shirt and a red hat for sun protection. (Red is my favorite color because it is very important in the plant world.)

I had tan pants with built-in kneepads. And lace-up leather work boots.

This outfit was designed for practical reasons.

My unruly, long curly hair was pulled back and secured by some kind of clip. I had magnifying glasses (like the elderly wear) for close-up inspection.

In my garden, in this uniform, I determined (through chemical analysis at the age of 7) that the brown flecks that appeared on the backyard furniture were bee poops.

I was astonished that more people had not figured this out before.

In an ideal world, I would have spent twenty-four hours a day conducting investigations.

But rest is critically important for development in young people.

I calculated my exact biorhythms and I needed 7 hours and 47 minutes of rest every night.

Not just because I was obsessed with the number 7.

Which was the case.

But because that's how my circadian rhythms were set. It's chemical.

Isn't everything?

I was told that I lived too much inside my head.

Maybe because of this, I haven't done that well at school and I've never had many friends.

But my garden gave me a window into other aspects of companionship.

When I was eight years old, a flock of wild, green-rumped parrots moved into the fishtail palm tree by the back wooden fence.

A pair built a nest and I was able to witness the arrival of the parrot babies.

Each one of those little birds had their own distinctive chirp.

I'm pretty sure only the mom green-rumped parrot and I knew this.

When the littlest parrot was pushed from the nest, I rescued the tiny creature, naming him Fallen.

With careful hand-feeding that in the beginning went around the clock, I was able to parrot-parent.

When Fallen was finally strong enough to fly, I reintroduced him back to his flock.

It was incredibly rewarding.

But it was also heartbreaking.

It has been my experience that rewarding and heartbreaking often go hand in hand.

In grade school, at Rose Elementary, I had one true companion.

Her name was Margaret Z. Buckle.

She made up the Z because she didn't have a middle name, and she had strong feelings about being seen as an individual.

But Margaret (don't ever call her Peggy) moved away the summer after fifth grade. Her mother is a petroleum engineer, and she got transferred to Canada.

Despite the distance, I thought that Margaret and I would stay really close.

And in the beginning it was like that.

But I guess people are a lot more open in Canada, because in Bakersfield it was just Margaret and me against the world.

Up there she has all kinds of friends.

Now, on the rare times when we correspond, she brings up things like a new sweater she got. Or a band she likes.

She doesn't want to talk about chiropterophily, which is the pollination of plants by bats.

She's moved on.

Who can blame her?

With Margaret in Canada, I was hoping that Sequoia Middle School would open up new avenues for friendship.

It hasn't worked out that way.

I'm small for my age, but I had a lot of anticipation about becoming a "Sequoia Giant."

Just the fact that the place had a tree as a mascot seemed so promising.

The school was on the other side of town and it was supposed to give me a fresh start, since the kids from my elementary all went on to Emerson.

My parents got special permission from the district to move me there.

Mom and Dad believed that I'd never found a teacher who truly understood me. I think it was more accurate to say that I'd never understood any of my teachers.

There's a difference.

Right before school began in the fall, the anticipation I felt was like waiting for my Amorphophallus paeoniifolius to bloom.

I went through a period of obsessively cultivating rare corpse flowers.

My initial attraction was to their strange-looking blossom.

The deep purplish red petals resemble sheets of velvet fabric that could line a casket. And the long, aggressive, yellowy stigma jutting from the center is like a jaundiced old man's finger.

But the plant's reputation comes from its smell. Because when the bloom opens, it's like having a dead body pop up from the soil.

The stink is simply indescribably disgusting. I mean, it really takes some adjustment.

No animal wants to get close, much less munch on the reeking, exotic, wine-colored blossom.

It's a reverse perfume.

I believed that going to middle school would be life-changing. I saw myself as the rare plant, prepared to unfurl hidden layers.

But I truly hoped that I wouldn't stink up the place.

I tried to fit in.

I researched teenagers, which was interesting because I was close to becoming one.

I read about teenage driving, teenage runaways, and teenage dropout rates. And it was a shocker.

But none of the research provided much enlightenment on my number one area of real interest:

Teenage friendship.

If the media is to be believed, teenagers are too busy breaking laws and trying to kill themselves and the people around them to form any bonds of attachment.

Unless, of course, those bonds produce a teenage pregnancy.

The literature had a lot of information on that.

Right before I started middle school, I had a physical.

The exam went much, much, much better than expected because for the first time I had an actual medical issue.

I had been waiting for twelve long years for this to happen.

I needed glasses.

Yes, the level of correction was slight.

And yes, it could have been brought on in part by eye-strain (apparently I focus too long on something right in front of me, like a book or a computer screen, and I don't look away into the distance and refocus enough).

So I congratulated myself on this achievement because I had been hoping for some form of myopia, and now I had it.

After the exam we went to the ophthalmologist and I picked out my eyeglasses. I was drawn to frames that looked like what Gandhi wore.

They were round, wire-rimmed, and very "old-school," according to the woman who deals with that part of the process.

They were perfect because I was going forward in the brave new world in peace.

A week before the first day of classes, I made another big decision.

We were having breakfast, and I swallowed a large bite of my Healthy-Start meal, which consists of beet greens topped with flax seeds (both homegrown), and then I said:

"I have figured out what I'm going to wear for my first day at Sequoia."

My father was at the sink, sneaking a bite of a doughnut. I did my best to keep junk food away from these people, but they covered up a lot of their eating habits.

My dad quickly swallowed a piece of his fudge puppy and asked:

"And what will that be?"

I was pleased.

"I'll be wearing my gardening outfit."

Dad must have taken too large of a bite, because it sounded like the fudge doughnut was caught in his throat. He managed to say:

"Are you sure about that?"

Of course I was sure. But I stayed low-key.

"Yes. But I won't put binoculars around my neck—if that's what you're concerned about."

My mom, who up until this point was unloading the dishwasher, turned around. I could see her face. She looked pained. Like maybe she had just put away a whole load of dirty dishes, which is something that had happened before.

Her face smoothed out and she said:

"What an interesting idea, honey. But I'm wondering . . . will people make the connection? Maybe it's better to wear a brighter color. Like something red. You love red."

They didn't get it.

The first day at middle school was a chance to make a new introduction. I needed to convey to the group a sense of my identity, while keeping a few of the basic elements of my character under wraps.

I couldn't stop myself from explaining:

"I'm making a statement about my commitment to the natural world."

I saw them exchange quick looks.

My dad had fudge frosting on his front teeth, but I wasn't going to point this out, especially after he said:

"Of course. You are so right."

I looked down into my breakfast bowl and began counting the flax seeds, multiplying them by 7s.

7 14 21 28 35 42 **49** 56 63 70
77 84 **91 98** 105 112 **119** 126 133 **140**
147 154 161 168 175 **182 189** 196 203 210
217 224 **231 238** 245 252 **259 266 273** 280
287 294 301 308 **315 322 329** 336 343 350

357 **364** **371** 378 385 392 *399* **406** **413** 420

427 434 441 448 **455** **462** *469* 476 483 490

497 **504** **511** 518 525 532 *539* 546 **553** **560**

It's an escape technique.

The next afternoon, a *Teen Vogue* magazine just appeared on my bed.

All of these publications at that time of year centered on going "Back to School."

On the cover a teenage girl with hair the color of a banana had the widest smile that I have ever seen. The headline read:

DOES YOUR OUTFIT SAY WHAT YOU WANT IT TO?

No one took responsibility for putting it there.

chapter 4

M y parents made a few more strange suggestions
before the first day of classes began.

I decided that they both must have been traumatized
as teenagers.

On that first morning at an entirely new school, I packed
my red, wheeled luggage (designed for the frequent business traveler but purchased to transport my books and
supplies), and we headed out the door to the car.

My father and mother both insisted on dropping me
off. But neither parent, per my direction, would accom-
pany me inside.

I had reviewed the floor plan of the actual buildings,
memorized everything from the ceiling heights to emergency exits to electrical outlet locations.

I was pre-enrolled in English, math, Spanish, physical
education, social studies, and science.

With the exception of P.E., I knew a lot about the subjects.

I had calculated the amount of time I needed to walk
the halls, as well as the cubic feet of the storage closets.

I could recite the entire Sequoia student handbook.

As we pulled out of the driveway, I was anxious, but I knew for certain one thing:

I was ready for middle school.

I was wrong.

The place was so loud.

The girls were shrieking and the boys were physically attacking each other.

At least that's how it appeared.

I hated to remove my red panama hat.

It was my signature color, but the hat was designed, after all, for sun protection.

I had only taken four steps into the mob when a girl approached.

She came right up to me and said:

"The toilet in the second stall is broken. It's totally gross."

She waved her arm in the direction of more meat-eaters and then she was gone.

I took a moment to process her statement.

Was she giving me some kind of informational heads-up?

I could see her talking to two girls next to a row of lockers and she didn't have the same intensity.

I looked through the swarm and I saw a slight, dark-haired man pulling a wheeled cart. It was loaded with cleaning supplies. Two mops were attached to the back.

I stared at him and realized that he and I were dressed alike.

But he was pulling a cleaning trolley, not luggage with wheels that have a 360-degree rotating option.

And then I had a distressing thought: It was possible that the girl believed I was some kind of maintenance worker.

I lasted less than three hours.

The place made me severely nauseated. For health and safety reasons, I went to the office and insisted on calling home.

I waited outside at the curb and just the sight of my mom's car in the distance made it easier to breathe.

When I climbed inside, my mother instantly said:

"First days are always hard."

If I were the kind of person who cried, I'm sure that I would have, but that's not in my character. I almost never cry. Instead, I just nodded and stared out the window.

I can disappear like that into myself.

Once we were home, I spent the rest of the afternoon in my garden.

I didn't till the soil or weed the flowerbeds or try to graft a tree limb; I sat in the shade and listened to my Japanese language instruction.

That night, I found myself staring out the window at the sky and counting by 7s for what ended up being a new record.

I tried to roll with it.

But what I learned and what was being taught had no intersection.

While my teachers labored over the rigors of their chosen subject, I sat in the back, pretty much bored out of my mind. I knew the stuff, so instead I studied the other students.

I came to a few conclusions about the middle school experience:

Clothing was very important.

In my opinion, if the world were perfect, everyone would wear lab coats in educational settings, but that obviously was not happening.

The average teenager was willing to wear very uncomfortable attire.

From my observation, the older you get, the more you like the word *cozy*.

That's why most of the elderly wear pants with elastic waistbands. If they wear pants at all. This may explain why grandparents are in love with buying grandkids pajamas and bathrobes.

The outfits worn by my fellow students were, in my opinion, either way too tight or way too loose.

Apparently having something that actually fits was not acceptable.

Haircuts and accessories were defining.

The color black was very popular.

Some of the students worked very hard to stand out.

Others put as much effort into blending in.

Music was some kind of religion.

It seemed to bring people together, and tear them apart. It identified a group, and apparently it prescribed ways to behave and react.

Interaction between the male species and the female species was varied and intense and highly unpredictable.

There was more touching than I thought there would be.

Some students had no inhibitions whatsoever.

No attention was paid to nutrition.

The word *deodorant* was not yet understood by over half of the boys.

And the word *awesome* was overused.

I was only 7 days into my latest educational misadventure when I walked into English class to find Mrs. Kleinsasser making an announcement:

"This morning everyone will be taking a standardized

test administered to all students in the state of California. On your desk you have a booklet and a number two pencil. Do not open the booklets until I give you instructions to do so."

Mrs. Kleinsasser signaled that she was ready and she started a clock.

And suddenly I decided to pay attention.

I took the pencil and began filling in the ovals with the answers.

In 17 minutes and 47 seconds I got up from my seat and walked to the front of the room, where I handed the answer form and the booklet to the teacher.

I slipped out the door and I thought it was possible that I heard the whole classroom whispering.

I received a perfect score.

I headed into Mrs. Kleinsasser's class a week later and she was waiting for me. She said:

"Willow Chance. Principal Rudin needs to see you."

My fellow middle schoolers buzzed at this news like pollen-soaked worker bees.

I went for the door, but at the last minute, I turned back.

It must have been obvious that I wanted to say something, because the room went quiet as I faced my classmates.

I found my voice and said:

"The human corpse flower has blossomed."

I'm almost certain no one got it.

I took a seat in Principal Rudin's office, which was much less impressive than I had hoped.

The anxious woman leaned on her desk, and her brow knitted into a strange pattern of angled, intersecting lines.

I felt certain that if I stared long enough, I would find a math theory in the woman's forehead.

But the lines rearranged themselves before I could work out the dynamic, and the principal said:

"Willow, do you know why you're here?"

I made the decision not to answer, hoping that might cause the skin above her eyes to again knit up.

The administrator didn't blink as she stared right at me.

"You cheated."

I found myself answering:

"I didn't cheat at anything."

Principal Rudin exhaled.

"Your file shows that you were identified several years ago as having high aptitude. Your teachers report no evidence of that. No one in the state got a perfect test score."

I could feel my face grow warm. I said:

"Really?"

But what I wanted to do was shout out:

"Your left elbow displays the fifth form of psoriasis—an erythrodermic condition characterized by intense redness in large patches. A course of 2.5% cortisone cream application combined with regulated exposure to sunlight—without sunburn, of course—would be my recommendation for relief."

But I didn't.

I had very little experience with authority. And zero experience as a practicing physician.

So I didn't defend myself.

I just clammed up.

What followed was a one-sided 47-minute-long interrogation.

The principal, unable to prove the deception, but certain that it had happened, finally let me go.

But not before she put in a formal request for me to see a behavioral counselor at the district main offices.

That's where the real problem kids were sent.

My counselor's name was Dell Duke.

chapter 5

dell duke

An ignoramus shoots at the wrong thing,
and hits it.

❧

Dell Duke could not believe that he had ended up in the sprawling agricultural community.

He had daydreamed bigger than this.

Delwood was his mother's last name and he'd been saddled with it as a first name at birth. But thankfully, no one had ever called him Delwood.

He was Dell from the start.

While Dell hated his first name, he took some measure of pride in Duke.

Only a few relatives knew that two generations before, the name had been Doufinakas, but his Greek ancestor George, as far as Dell was concerned, had done the right thing.

Dell hinted to anyone who would listen that his family had something to do with starting a university. And they had at one point worn a crown.

Early on, Dell Duke had wanted to be a doctor because he liked TV shows with heroic people who saved lives every week while showing off perfect teeth and great haircuts.

Plus *Dr. Dell Duke* sounded good. It had three *D*'s. Which sounded better than two.

And so Dell studied biology in college, which didn't go well because he couldn't store facts.

They shifted and then moved and quickly evaporated from his conscious mind.

And if they were buried somewhere in his unconscious, he had no access to that area of thought.

So by his second semester, he'd changed his major for the fourth time, moving from the hard sciences to the soft sciences.

Dell finally graduated, on the six-and-a-half-year plan, with a degree in psychology.

From there, after a lot of searching, he got a job at an assisted-living center, where he was the activities director.

Dell was let go after only three months.

The elderly didn't like him. He lacked true compassion and he had no stomach for their health problems. On more than one occasion he was seen running from the activities room in a full-blown panic.

Dell was too afraid to work with prison inmates and so he set his sights on the public school system.

Dell went to night classes and after three more years

got a certification for adolescent counseling, and that put him on the path to work in education.

But no one was hiring.

Dell sent out literally hundreds of résumés, and after three years working as a bar-back, carrying tubs of used glasses to the surly dishwashers, he finally added some bogus counseling work experience to his résumé and got a bite.

Bakersfield.

On paper, it looked incredible.

The map showed that he would be in Southern California. He imagined a life of surfboards with groups of tanned people eating medium-spiced corn chips on his seaside balcony.

But the Central Valley had entire months where the temperature hit 100 degrees every single day. It was flat and dry and land-locked.

Bakersfield was no Malibu.

It wasn't even Fresno.

Dell accepted the position, packed up his barely drivable Ford, and headed south.

He didn't have a going away party when he left Walla Walla, Washington, because no one cared that he was leaving.

As a counselor for the Bakersfield City school district, Dell's job was to handle the difficult cases.

And by that, the district meant the middle school students who got into trouble, almost exclusively for behavioral issues. These were the kids who caused enough trouble to be dealt with off site.

A typical day for Dell consisted of reviewing dozens of e-mails filed weekly from principals.

Some of the students were reported because they had turned physically violent. They were kids who targeted other kids. This meant an automatic suspension if the incident was on school grounds.

You could beat up someone, but you had to make sure it wasn't in the school cafeteria or the parking lot.

The sidewalk was a perfectly fine place.

Other cases involved truancy.

It struck Dell as ironic that there were kids who didn't go to school, and they would be punished for not attending with the threat of being kicked out altogether.

In addition to the violent students and the no-shows, there were the kids who did drugs and the ones who stole things.

But these cases never made it in to see Dell. The system took care of the young criminals on its own. (Dell resented that he didn't get face time with the real bullies.

They had a lot of personality, and could be quite entertaining.)

It was the rest of the screwups who were left to counseling.

There were three educational therapists who handled all the cases. Dell was the fresh hire after Dickie Winkleman, who had served for forty-two years, retired. (Dell never met Dickie Winkleman, but from what he heard, the guy was a broken man when he finally walked out the door.)

As the new guy on the block, Dell was given the kids who the other two counselors didn't want.

The way Dell saw it: He got the losers of the losers.

But Dell was okay with that because it wasn't like the students he saw would run and tell someone what a crummy job he was doing. They had already turned against the system before they arrived.

Score!

Dell was now in his mid-thirties, and while he wasn't insightful or even thoughtful, he knew that this counseling job in Bakersfield would make or break him.

But Dell had always had an issue with organization. He couldn't throw things away because he had trouble figuring out what had value and what didn't.

Plus he liked the comfort of possessions. If he couldn't

belong to something, at least something belonged to him.

Looking through Dickie Winkleman's old files before the whole system had gone electronic, Dell found that Dickie had put kids in categories.

It seemed that the counselor had organized the students in terms of three things:

Activity level

Patience

Ability to pay attention

Counselor Winkleman had elaborate notes and wrote up painstakingly detailed reports where he made an effort to quantify his students' abilities and deficiencies.

Dell was impressed, and horrified.

There was no way he was going to try to imitate what Winkleman had done. It looked like way too much work.

Dell would have to come up with his own way of sorting through the weeds of messed-up students.

It only took him three months on the job to get the Dell Duke Counseling System in shape.

He placed all of the kids he saw into four groups of THE STRANGE.

First, there were the MISFITS.

Then the ODDBALLS.

Next were the LONE WOLVES.

And finally, the WEIRDOS.

Of course, Dell wasn't supposed to give the kids any kind of classifications, but what good is an organizing system without methods of separation?

Labels were important. And they were very effective. It was just too crazy to think of these kids on an individual basis.

The way the Dell Duke Counseling System broke it down, the Misfits were the kooky kids who just couldn't help but dress different and act like fish out of water.

The Misfits had no power dynamic. And some of them may have been dropped as babies. The Misfits, in all likelihood, were *trying* to fit in, but just couldn't.

His next group, the Oddballs, were different from the Misfits because the Oddballs were more original and usually somehow ahead of the curve.

They *liked* being odd. The Oddballs contained the artists and musicians. They had a tendency to be show-offs and eat spicy food. They were usually late, often wore the color orange, and weren't good with finances.

And then there were the Lone Wolves.

This group had the mavericks. They thought of themselves as protestors or rebels.

The Lone Wolf was often an angry wolf, whereas a Misfit was often calm and contented. And the Oddballs were just out to a lunch where they made their own sand-wiches.

Finally, in Dell's classification of the Strange, there were the Weirdos.

The Weirdos included the Zombies, those kids who stared straight ahead and gave back nothing no matter how hard someone tried to pry emotion out of them.

The Weirdos could be counted on to chew bits of their own stringy hair and fixate, non-blinking, on a dirt spot on the carpeting while a fire blazed right behind them.

Weirdos were fingernail-biters and liked to scratch themselves. They had secrets and were probably late to be toilet trained. The bottom line was that Weirdos were just plain weird because of their unpredictability. And in Dell's opinion, they could be dangerous. It was always best to simply let a Weirdo be.

Game.

Set.

Match.

Because Dell's files could end up in the hands of people in higher places than his windowless room in one-half of a converted trailer on the property of the school district administration offices, he made a code for his unique system, which he thought of as FGS, which stood for:

THE FOUR GROUPS OF THE STRANGE.

FGS broke down to:

```
1 = MISFITS
2 = ODDBALLS
3 = LONE WOLVES
4 = WEIRDOS
```

He also, after much thought, color coded his unique system.

```
MISFITS were yellow.
ODDBALLS were purple.
LONE WOLVES were green.
WEIRDOS were red.
```

Dell then changed the font color on his personal files in his computer to correspond with his categorization.

This allowed him at a glance to know what he was dealing with.

The name Eddie Von Snodgrass appeared onscreen and before the jumpy kid in the oversized jacket had even slid into his seat, Dell knew that he could secretly surf his computer for forty-two minutes and nod his head every once in a while.

Lone Wolves didn't need much feedback because they liked to rant and rave.

And so, while Eddie V. went off on the chemical taste of soda in plastic bottles, Dell checked out a website that sold bobble-head baseball player dolls at very affordable prices.

And Dell didn't even like sports memorabilia!

But the Duke Counseling System was up and working, even if Dell was not.

Because once a kid had been evaluated, Dell could complete the district's form in a flash, giving everyone in a specific category the same rating.

Months passed. Dell kept the kids moving in and out. The trains full of the Strange ran on time.

And then on the afternoon that Willow Chance came to see him, all of his categorization ground to a halt, like a fork thrown into the gears of outdated machinery.

chapter 6

⟨≈⟩

I sat in the airless office/trailer and stared at Mr. Dell
Duke.

His head was very round. Most human heads are not
round. Very, very few, in fact, have any real spherical quality.

But this chubby, bearded man with bushy eyebrows,
and sneaky eyes, was the exception.

He had thick, curly hair and ruddy skin and it looked
to me as if he was at least of partial Mediterranean origin.

I was very interested in the diet of these countries.

The combination of olive oil, hearty vegetables, and
cheese that comes from goat's milk, mixed with decent
servings of fish and meat, had been shown in numerous
studies to promote longevity.

But Mr. Dell Duke did not look so healthy.

In my opinion, he wasn't getting enough exercise. I saw
that he had a substantial belly under his loose-fitting shirt.

And weight carried around the middle is more deleteri-
ous than extra pounds in the butt.

Yet, culturally speaking, today men with big butts are

considered less desirable than a man with a potbelly, which is no doubt wrong from an evolutionary point of view.

I would have liked to take his blood pressure.

He started by saying that he didn't want to discuss my test scores.

But that's all he talked about.

For a long time, I didn't say a single word.

And that made him talk more.

About a lot of nothing.

It was hot in his stuffy little office and as I stared at him, I could see that he was sweating up a storm.

Even his beard was starting to look wet.

He was getting more and more agitated. As he spoke, small dots of saliva lodged in the corners of his mouth.

They were foamy and white.

Mr. Dell Duke had a large jar of jelly beans on his desk.

He didn't offer me any.

I don't eat candy, but I was fairly certain he did.

I guessed that he had the jelly beans to make it look like he was offering kids a treat, but in actuality he never did and went on his own jelly-bean-eating binges.

I considered calculating how many were in the glass container.

The volume of one jelly bean = $h(pi)(d/2)^2$ = 2cm x 3 $(1.5cm/2)^2$ = 3.375 or 27/8 cubic centimeters.

But jelly beans aren't really perfect cylinders. They are irregular.

So this formula was not accurate.

It would have been more fun for me to try to count them by 7s.

I hadn't told my parents about meeting Principal Psoriasis from Sequoia.

Or that I would have to see some kind of school parole officer named Dell Duke.

I'm not sure why.

It had been their idea to move schools, and I wanted them to think things were going well.

Or as well as possible.

So I was now officially duplicitous.

It didn't feel good.

The middle school years were supposed to be (according to the literature) about an emotional separation from parents. I figured lying was laying a good groundwork for that.

But it was as if I'd eaten something that was giving me

indigestion. And that burning sensation extended beyond my stomach and moved upward, where it lodged in my neck.

Right where I swallowed.

My parents didn't know any of my test-taking drama at Sequoia because I destroyed the evidence.

I erased the message from the school that was on our home phone voicemail. My parents always forgot to check it, so that wasn't a big deal.

But what was more deceitful is that I hacked into my mom's e-mail and answered the principal's note about going to see a district counselor.

So I would just have to put up with this stomach queasiness, because I deserved it.

The round-head counselor/warden finally stopped talking.

He was worn out.

He folded his short arms defensively over his ball of a belly, and then after more sweaty silence (on both of our parts), he had an actual idea:

"I'm gonna say a word, and then you say the first word that comes into your head. I'm not saying the word as a question—it's something else. Let's try to do this very quickly."

He sucked in a lot of air and added:

"Think of it as a game."

Dell Duke didn't know that my experience in this arena was very limited.

But I have found myself to be shockingly competitive.

For the first time since I stepped into the room, I felt mild enthusiasm.

He wanted to play a word game. I was certain that I could beat him in chess in fewer than six moves. But I have only played against a computer, and not often, because chess is one of those things that can become obsessive.

I know.

I once played for twenty hours straight and experienced signs of mild psychosis.

Mr. Dell Duke leaned forward in his chair and dramatically said:

"Chocolate."

I was interested in the benefits of chocolate and I said:

"Antioxidant."

He then tapped his foot, like he was accelerating in a car, and said:

"Piano."

I said:

"Concerto."

The day before, I had heard a kid at school shout to a group of boys in the hall:

"Game on!"

I wanted to shout that now, but it didn't feel appropriate.

Mr. Dell Duke tried to write down what he and I said, but he was struggling.

Fortunately, he gave up and decided to just play the game.

He said "space." I said "time."

He said "dark." I said "matter."

He said "big." I said "bang."

He said "car." I said "tography."

He said "mouse." I said "wireless."

He said "white." I said "corpuscle."

He said "single." I said "source."

He said "seed." I said "embryo."

He said "pie."

I said "3.141592653589793238462643383327."

But I said the number very, very, very fast and I stopped on the second 7 because of course that was my favorite number.

Mr. Dell Duke then loudly shouted:

"You animal!"

It scared me.

I don't like loud things. I was silent for a long time, but then finally managed to find my voice.

I said:

"Lemur."

And then his eyes grew sort of dazed for an instant and he mumbled:

"Female lemurs are in charge of the troop."

This was an accurate statement.

If there is conflict in the group, the female lemurs are the ones who fight it out. Because of this, the female leader gets the best food and the preferred sleeping area.

I now looked at him hard.

Not everyone knows that a lemur is a primate found only on the island of Madagascar.

It was possible he was not the toadstool that he appeared to be.

He then ran both of his hands through his curly mop of hair, and that made it double in size.

That has happened to my hair before.

So I understood.

I left the meeting confused.

I knew that he knew that I was different.

Mr. Dell Duke wasn't friend material because he was

the wrong age and, female lemurs notwithstanding, we appeared to have absolutely nothing in common.

But as I walked away from the district headquarters parking lot, I decided I would come back and see him again.

Mr. Dell Duke was testing me.

But not in the way he thought.

I believed he somehow needed me.

I liked the feeling.

That night at the dinner table, my mom and dad asked me how it was going at Sequoia.

I said:

"The experience is evolving."

My parents both smiled, but their eyes were still anxious. My mom's voice was tighter than usual as she said:

"Is there anyone special who you've enjoyed meeting?"

For the briefest moment, I questioned whether they knew about the aptitude test.

I took a bite of my artichoke soufflé and finished chewing before answering.

"I met someone who interests me."

My parents perked up. This was big news for them.

Mom tried not to appear too eager.

"Can you tell us more?"

I had to be careful here. If I didn't want a colossal stomachache, I had to use a version of the truth.

"This afternoon was my first encounter. Viewed as a clinical trial, I'm in Phase Zero, which is when micro-dosing takes place. I'll let you know how it develops."

And then I asked to be excused from the table.

Chapter 7

～

D ell didn't see many girls.
Boys got into a lot more trouble in school.

He had assumed that "Willow" was some kind of nickname. He figured it was really "Will-Low," which might have been gang slang.

Instead, seated across from him had been a twelve-year-old girl.

There was something not right about her.

He could see that from the beginning.

Her eyes darted around his small room and then came to rest on his stomach, which was rude.

He knew he was sweating, which was just part of who he was.

But he got the feeling that she was judging him.

That's not what this place was about.

He was the judger.

He needed to put her in a category of Strange as soon as possible so that he could disconnect from whatever was happening in the room.

Dell had glanced over at his computer to reread the e-mail he'd been sent from Principal Rudin.

The message said that the girl was some kind of cheater. He didn't get many of those.

So she was sneaky.

Well, so was he.

He'd get to the bottom of that.

She wasn't a Weirdo or a Lone Wolf or an Oddball or a Misfit.

But she *was* Super-Strange, that much he could figure out.

He talked and talked and talked and she just sat there, mute, staring at him, but he could tell that she was listening.

He asked questions, but she didn't answer them.

She was small, but also powerful.

She had some kind of energy or aura that was different.

None of his tricks, if he could even call them that, worked.

And then he remembered word association.

It was a technique that he knew the other counselors used because he'd heard them when the windows were open and the air conditioners weren't rattling.

Dell fell asleep every night with the television on.

He had hours of recorded broadcasts, because the sound of other people's voices, especially ones that weren't yelling at him, was a comfort.

But nothing made him fall asleep faster than something educational.

And that is why as the hour got late and Dell was looking to pack it in, he often went to the most boring thing that he'd ever recorded: a wildlife documentary on the animals of Madagascar.

Scientists had made the show. It was filled with facts and feelings, two things that Dell could live without.

If he was going to actually watch a nature documentary, the only kind that he could suffer through was one where a fierce predator took down a wide-eyed furball.

But he liked it when the furball could see it coming.

A good chase with a few near misses added tension to the eventual crime scene.

A male narrator with a deep, husky (almost evil) voice set the stage for the slaughter. The music surged.

And then *Bam!*

Done.

The Madagascar show had nothing like that. It focused on a group of monkeys who looked like squirrels in raccoon costumes.

There was nothing in this program of interest and Dell had fallen asleep to it many times since he came to Bakersfield.

He would not, could not, recall a single thing from the program other than what he had uttered to Willow at the end of their first session:

"Female lemurs are in charge of the troop."

As she gathered up her things and silently headed out the door, Dell realized that his somewhat hairy hands were both trembling.

He had never met a kid like this.

He quickly accessed the electronic file that he was required to complete after every interaction with a student.

But for the first time since his Four Groups of the Strange system went into operation, Dell put it aside and dug out Dickie Winkleman's three areas of evaluation:

Activity

Patience

Attention

Willow had the ability to pay attention.

She appeared to exhibit patience (she had listened to him drone on for the first half of the appointment).

But he could not rate her activity level.

Dell copied a paragraph from one of Dickie Winkleman's old files. It had been written for a kid named Wesley Ledbetter.

Dell wondered if Wesley's problem was that his name sounded like "Bed-wetter." That could certainly throw a person off.

It said that Wesley appeared to be normal, but needed further evaluation for possible anxiety issues.

In truth, Dell knew that the twelve-year-old with the large eyes (who had told him to have his blood pressure checked just before she left) was anything but normal.

And for the first time in his professional career, he was not just motivated.

He was almost inspired.

The counselor had to add a new group to his system.

He had to access the color wheel on his computer and feverishly attempt to create something that would look metallic.

Something that would stand out like oozing gold ink.

Because Dell Duke believed he had discovered a new category of the Strange:

GENIUS.

chapter 8

After I was removed from Mrs. Kleinsasser's class and taken to Principal Eczema's office, my teachers and the other students treated me differently.

A few of my classmates, assuming that I'm some kind of cheater, asked me for answers to tests.

An eighth grader with what looked to me like a full-on beard demanded my math homework from last Tuesday.

I was so startled that I gave him my entire binder, which I later found on top of the trash by the boys' bathroom near the gym.

He'd left half of a roll of breath mints inside, but I think it was an accident, not a gift.

I was surprised that I was looking forward to the long walk from Sequoia Middle School over to the district offices where I had my second meeting with Mr. Dell Duke.

Knowing that I had somewhere to go gave me a new sense of purpose.

Even if it meant again lying to my parents.

But it was easier to lie the second week than the first time around, which was sad.

I decided any behavior, good or bad, could become routine.

This was probably why people were able to empty porta potties or regulate the quality of canned cat food in factories with actual taste tests.

Now when the last bell rang, and the school suddenly exploded (because that's how it felt), I gathered up my things with new gusto. (I like the word *gusto*. It should be used more in daily life.)

The doors of the school flew open and the students burst from the building as if there had been some kind of toxic-waste spill inside.

I was now part of that.

I, too, had someplace to go and a limited amount of time to get there.

When I got to his office, I could see right away that Dell Duke was prepared in a different way.

He still looked as if he had slept for the last week in his clothes; but his beard had been trimmed, or at least washed.

And his very cluttered office had been straightened up.

However, what made me smile as I stood in the doorway was that I saw he now had a small silver frame on the side table behind his desk.

And in the picture frame, like some kind of lost relative, was a photo of a lemur.

He was nervous.

He struggled to make conversation, but then he finally just blurted out:

"What would you think about taking a test again—like the one you did at school?"

I decided that was why he was anxious, and so I put an end to it.

"I'll take one right now if you want."

This made him very happy.

He had a folder behind his desk with test booklets inside. He was suddenly all jumpy and I had to help him with the pencil and the timer.

I tried to explain that I wouldn't need the allotted fifty minutes.

He didn't believe me until I finished the first test in fourteen minutes.

After he corrected the exam, I removed another booklet from the pile and did that one in twelve minutes and 7 seconds.

If I could have had perfect test conditions—a room

with decent ventilation, and a glass of unsweetened green iced tea—I would have cut off another two minutes.

I got up to go, because my session was now over, and Dell Duke was smiling. Unbroken mouth expansion.

He said that I didn't miss a single question, on either test.

I said, in a very matter-of-fact way:

"Flawless."

Maybe he thought we were playing the word game, because he made a fist and pumped it like he was pulling down on a parachute cord (even though I'd never done that, I had an idea how enthusiastic one would be to pull the chute).

He then said in a voice that was too loud:

"Willow Chance!"

Mr. Dell Duke didn't want me to wait a week for our next meeting.

He thought that I should come again during his first open hour the next day.

He told me that he would bring a surprise to the meeting. I have never been big on surprises, but I didn't tell him.

I was planning on assessing the acidity of the soil in my garden for the rest of the week.

I worked hard to keep it at a pH of 6.5, but I agreed to return because he seemed to be very excited about the aptitude tests and I thought that he might be depressed.

It was possible that he was making some progress in his mental health condition by seeing me.

The next afternoon I was five minutes early and right away I knew that something was different.

The door to the trailer office was open, but not wide like usual. It was open only a slice.

So I looked inside and I didn't see Dell Duke. I saw two bodies.

But not dead bodies.

Alive.

I stepped back, but one of the two, the teenage girl, had seen me.

And she said:

"It's okay. You can come in."

I didn't know if I should do this.

The room was cramped and even though there was an extra chair, I felt like I was intruding.

But then the girl got up and pushed the door open all the way and said:

"We're almost out of here."

I could now see that an older boy was hunched over

a coloring book and he was very intently filling in the spaces.

I've never understood coloring books.

Either draw a picture, or don't. But why waste your time coloring in someone else's work?

I knew that Dell Duke saw other students from the school district, but the sight of the two older kids made me uncomfortable.

The girl suddenly said:

"My brother won't leave until he finishes his assignment. Sorry. His session was over ten minutes ago."

The boy shot the girl a hostile look, but returned to his feverish coloring. The girl then continued:

"Mr. Duke went to get a soda. At least that's what he said he was going to do. But he's been gone a long time, so I don't believe him."

I nodded, but didn't speak.

I admired the suspicion in the girl's statement and I now hoped that Dell Duke didn't walk through the door holding a Diet Pepsi.

I made a note to myself to talk to him about soft drinks.

Those beverages are not healthy.

I was tired from dodging the volleyball in gym class, and so I took the only other seat in Dell's office.

I didn't want to stare, but the teenage girl now at my side was visually very interesting.

Like me, she was someone impossible to easily peg in terms of ethnic background.

At first glance, she might have been African American. Her skin was dark; her hair was shiny black, and a bed of curls.

I kept my head facing forward and completely still, but moved my eyes into their corners to get a better look.

With this closer, peripheral examination, I suddenly wondered if the girl was a Native American.

I took great interest in the cultures of indigenous people.

What if this girl was a member of the Cahuilla tribe?

The Cahuilla lived in Southern California and once thrived in Bakersfield.

It was possible.

But not probable.

Suddenly I couldn't control myself. I turned to the girl next to me and asked:

"Do you speak Takic?"

chapter 9

mai & quang-ha

A leader gets everyone to shoot

in the same direction.

❧

Nguyen Thi Mai was fourteen years old and a freshman at Condon High School, which was on the other side of Bakersfield from where Willow Chance lived.

She had a brother named Nguyen Quang-ha who was a year older.

Quang-ha was a troublemaker.

Mai was not.

She was determined and deliberate in everything she did, and that quality attracted people to her.

Mai had true confidence. Or as she liked to see herself, she was born strong-willed, while a lot of the world was wishy-washy.

Adults didn't intimidate her, and neither did strangers of any age.

Because Mai, as her mother reminded people, was born in the year of the dragon; and that meant nobility and power and strength.

Starting the second week of class, on Thursday afternoons, the teenage kids caught a bus to the school district main offices for Quang-ha's appointment in Dell Duke's windowless mobile unit.

Mai had the bus fare, a bottle of water, and two snacks. Even though she was a year younger than her brother, she had long been his keeper.

Mai waited for Quang-ha to have his counseling session, and when he was finished, they went together to Happy Polish Nails.

This was the salon that their mother operated.

Mai knew, of course, that she and her brother stood out in Bakersfield.

Her mother had been born in Vietnam from a father who was a black American soldier. Because of this, Mai's mother, who was named Dung, had been an outcast.

When the U.S. government gave teenage Dung a chance, she had left home and gone halfway around the world to California. In the next ten years, she had two children with a man originally from Mexico (who had left soon after Mai was born to see his sick brother, and had never come back).

Dung had changed her name to Pattie once she found

out what it meant in English. But even though she had been in the United States for twenty-one years, some of her mail still came addressed to Dung. Her kids didn't appreciate it.

⁕

Dell had ignored (even more than usual) his regularly scheduled cases.

He gave the pest known as Quang-ha a geometric coloring book and commanded that the kid complete three pages.

Dell was surprised to see that, instead of complaining, the hostile teenager actually looked enthused to employ colored pencils to fill in blank spaces.

Being careful that no one was watching, Dell then got in his car and took off. He had fifty minutes to take care of his business.

Dell Duke returned to the room without a can of soda, but with a pet carrier. His voice was strangely high-pitched and harsh as he said:

"Quang-ha, you should be done by now. I told you to leave at ten till four."

Quang-ha continued coloring and didn't even bother to look up.

Mai and Willow Chance both fixated on the jail-like

front panel of the beige plastic crate, where they saw an extremely large orange cat.

Dell Duke was insistent:

"You have to go. My next appointment is here!"

Quang-ha kept working the mustard-colored pencil as if he was getting bonus money for every stroke.

This shouldn't have surprised Dell because the kid was in counseling for not following classroom instruction and having control problems.

But *Dell* looked like the one with a control problem. His face flushed deep red and he put the pet carrier down on his desk as he raised his voice.

"Done! Finished! No more coloring!"

Willow seemed to be sucked back into her chair.

And when that happened, Mai got to her feet. She was some kind of wild tiger unleashed into the airless room.

"Don't you raise your voice at us! He didn't do anything wrong. If my brother wants to finish the picture, he'll *finish the picture!*"

She took in a deep breath and continued.

"He was supposed to have a counseling session, but you were gone the whole time. That's not right! You are late for your next appointment with this little girl here.

And *that's* not right either! And here's something else to chew on: I don't think you're allowed to have animals on school property. We could turn you in for that!"

chapter 10

∿

I felt my blood pressure rise.

But in a good way.

The exotic-looking teenager standing in front of me was bold.

She was yelling at Mr. Dell Duke and the tone of her voice demanded that the world listen as she stood up for her brother and for me.

It was there, in the small, stuffy trailer on the edge of the baking-hot blacktop of the Bakersfield school district parking lot, that I found an older girl who was disappointing only in her failure to speak the language of the mostly obliterated Cahuilla people.

I found Mai Nguyen.

Dell Duke stared at us but he didn't say anything.

Instead he pulled the only rabbit he had out of a hat, which happened to be a cat from a cage.

He gave us all a wobbly smile and opened the metal door of the plastic pet carrier.

Then he said:

"This is my cat, Cheddar. I thought you might like to meet him."

So this was my surprise.

I had said that my father was allergic to pet hair, which was why I couldn't have a dog or a cat or even a pygmy goat.

This was Dell's attempt to please me. To bond. He brought in his cat. It was strange, but right then in that room, what wasn't?

The cat took several (in what looked like slow motion) steps onto the desk. I knew that cats behaved in this casual way because they weren't needy.

They didn't run and greet a person and slobber with joy.

They didn't look for validation or recognition.

They didn't fetch or cower or make big-eyed faces that say: "Love me, please."

Their failure to care wasn't just appealing, but seductive.

Because cats made you try.

We all watched as Cheddar sauntered across the desktop, rubbing his freakishly big body against the three shelves of the in-and-out box (where Dell Duke had piled official-looking paperwork that I suddenly felt certain he later simply dumped unread in the large storage closet that was behind his desk).

The huge cat then took a few sniffs and found the whole place not very satisfying.

With no obvious provocation, he leaped down to the floor and bounced right out of the building like a bright-colored, fur-covered soccer ball.

We watched as Cheddar hit the parking lot running, and in moments the fat cat had disappeared.

For 37 straight minutes, we all looked under cars, behind hedges, and around the buildings of the school district administration headquarters for the missing hunk of Cheddar.

But he was not to be found.

Dell claimed that he felt bad about this, but oddly it seemed that Mai and I felt much worse.

Finally, after agreeing to stop our search, we all returned to Dell's office to make LOST CAT flyers.

Dell didn't have any photos of his cat, which also struck me as strange because from everything that I'd read, photographing a pet seemed to be where most animal owners found their greatest joy.

But the problem was solved when Quang-ha drew a perfect pencil sketch of Cheddar, which then served as the centerpiece of the LOST CAT—PLEASE HELP—REWARD OFFERED flyer.

Dell wouldn't list an exact reward amount.

I believe that economic incentive is crucial as a motivator, especially in a consumer-driven society.

But I didn't argue the point.

We gathered around the copying machine in the main office and watched together as the image was reproduced.

It was here that I was able to identify a new sensation.

I have never been part of a true group effort with older kids.

And while we hadn't been successful in finding Dell Duke's lost cat named Cheddar, I couldn't help but experience a kind of accomplishment as I stood next to fourteen-year-old Mai and her surly big brother.

I was not pretending to be anyone but myself, and they still accepted me into their troop.

I felt human.

That was the only way I could describe it.

Mr. Dell Duke drove us home.

He said that he had to take me first and I assumed that this was because it would be inappropriate for him to be alone with a kid in his vehicle.

Parents had to give permission for students to be off school grounds with anyone who works for the district.

But I didn't want to raise any red flags, even though that was my signature color.

For a moment, I drifted off into my head, but not with thoughts about something like cellular structure.

I found myself imagining the place where Mai and Quang-ha lived.

Maybe it was a home with a chronically ill relative who was interested in regular examination by a young person who would listen endlessly to ailments and take precise notes.

Or perhaps Mai's family had an apartment with a roof-deck that housed an amateur self-constructed observatory with a shockingly powerful reflecting telescope.

Sitting in the backseat, I wanted to exchange vital contact information with this older and intriguing girl named Mai.

In a blink of pure fantasy, I suddenly saw myself walking away from Dell Duke's grimy car with a tiny glass vial of her blood sample for genome sequencing.

Because even though Mai said during the cat search that her mother came from Vietnam, I hadn't completely given up on the idea that she could have something to do with the Cahuilla tribe.

This was one of my secrets. When I was younger, I imagined that I was an Indian princess.

Looking out the car window to the street that I'd known my whole life, I understood that origins were so important.

Even if you didn't know your own.

I was energized.

Once I was home, I went into the kitchen and fixed myself a drink of hot water mixed with a tablespoon of honey (from my backyard beehive) and a tablespoon of my own homemade vinegar (made from tart apples, brown sugar, and distilled water).

As I sipped the tangy beverage, I was certain that the day, despite the loss of the counselor's cat, had been a triumph.

Having a friend—even one who was older and went to high school—would open a door for me into another world.

That afternoon I made a decision.

I would learn everything possible about lost cats and Vietnam.

It felt as if I were going up and over some kind of barrier after spending too long hitting the thing straight on.

chapter 11

M ai watched as Willow got out of the backseat and headed up the driveway, pulling her wheeled luggage behind her.

Quang-ha mumbled:

"Someone should tell her to get a backpack."

Mai shot him a hard look, which she knew would keep her brother quiet.

She could see that the strange girl's house had been painted the color of the shrimp curry that her mother made. It was a bold yellow that stuck out in the drab neighborhood.

But what really interested Mai was behind the house.

Because it was very green back there.

On one side, a stand of timber bamboo jutted up three stories high. On the other edge of the property, a tall palm tree and several smaller, bluish silver eucalyptus trees trembled together in the late-afternoon wind.

Staring at the house and the properties next door, it looked to Mai like there was a jungle behind where Willow lived.

No one else had that. Not in a neighborhood that spent two hundred days a year without rain.

Maybe, she theorized, the girl's parents owned a plant nursery.

Her brother didn't seem at all interested in Willow, or her house, but Dell stared intently with his nose almost touching the glass as Willow removed a key from a zipped pocket in her carry-on luggage.

Any regular little kid would have then turned and waved back, or done something to acknowledge the people in the waiting car.

But Willow simply unlocked the door and slid inside, disappearing into the shadows of the curry-colored house as if she were suddenly invisible.

It was intriguing.

Once Willow was gone, Mai watched as Dell Duke jerked his car out of park, hitting the gas pedal so quickly that the Ford lurched forward like a broken carnival ride.

Her eyes narrowed in suspicion.

So he was *that* eager to get rid of them?

Interesting.

She hadn't had a very good opinion of the counselor, but in the last hour she had been feeling bad about his lost cat.

Now she was quickly returning to her original position: Dell Duke was not a natural at his job.

After Dell dropped off the troublemaker and his flame-throwing sister, he headed home.

The route took him directly by the school district offices and that was when he saw Cheddar sitting in the still-hot sun on top of a once green Dumpster at the south side of the parking lot.

Dell didn't even brake to get a better look.

There were rats on the property. That was just a fact.

As far as Dell was concerned, Cheddar could pull his own weight back there. And maybe shed a pound or two in the process.

Dell had picked up the cat after reading a notice online about a lost pet.

It wasn't a shelter, so he didn't have to pay any fees. He just claimed the fleabag and even took the plastic cat carrier that the old lady offered.

The woman seemed thrilled to be reuniting the cat with the owner. Dell almost felt bad.

Still, he was going to dump the LOST CAT flyers in the trash. He had promised the kids that he'd post them, but that was just to keep them in their shoes. They'd been pretty anxious about losing Cheddar.

The flyers were on the passenger-side floorboard of the car.

Now, as he waited at a traffic light, he had to admit that the drawing, coupled with the imaginative and dedicated coloring that Quang-ha had done earlier in the afternoon, was disturbing.

The kid was a Lone Wolf.

He was coded green.

It was just wrong for the delinquent to have any artistic talent.

But anyone could see from the picture of Cheddar that the surly kid had some kind of visual sense.

Dell made a note to change Quang-ha's category.

He was going to be moved to purple, for Oddball.

Dell found himself wondering if all kinds of assumptions were questionable.

And that was Strange indeed.

Once in his possession-choked apartment, Dell peeled off his stinky shirt and poured himself a tall glass of red wine.

He next shoved a frozen meat loaf, which was supposed to be low in calories, into the microwave.

The box claimed it served three people.

He was trying to diet, but he always found himself eating the whole thing.

Dell then maneuvered around his heaps of junk, and

took a seat on his patio furniture, which he used indoors in his living room.

He was surprised people didn't realize that a decent chaise longue was much easier to move, yet still as comfortable as a couch.

Most outdoor recliners had wheels for mobility, and you could hose off the cushion if you spilled a bowl of salsa—and who didn't on occasion?

Under ordinary circumstances Dell would have turned on the TV to some kind of reality show, and after consuming the meat loaf and enough wine, he would have fallen asleep, usually with his mouth open, which inevitably served as a spout for pink-tinged saliva.

The saliva would have stained regular furniture, but it went right through the plastic weave of the lawn chair, which was another plus.

Dell would wake up hours later and if he had the energy, make his way through the maze of his possessions to his bedroom, where he would crawl into a sleeping bag.

This was another one of his lifestyle choices.

Once a year he dropped the sleeping bag off at the dry cleaner's. Forget the sheets and blankets and comforters and duvet covers! Modern life provided enough challenges without throwing in making the bed.

But tonight Dell didn't fall asleep in a small puddle of drool. He lay awake in his sleeping bag, which he believed had the smell of a brown bear (a mix of wet fur and dead leaves and empty wine bottles), thinking about the events of his day and the genius kid.

had a plan.

I'd been walking to Mr. Dell Duke's office for my appointments, but now that I knew Mai and her brother would be there before me, I wanted to get there early.

So I went online the following week and ordered a taxi to pick me up at the curb when school was over.

This was a very brave and daring act for me.

I waited in front of the sign that said SEQUOIA GIANTS, and the taxi arrived right on time.

I believed we were off to a good start.

I pulled my wheeled luggage to the cab door and leaned in through the open window as I said:

"I would like the number of your taxi license and to see proof of your compliance with brake and headlight adjustment requirements."

The driver's name was Jairo Hernandez, and he had been driving for Mexicano Taxi for seven years.

I was nervous, but he seemed nervous as well.

He did not appear, however, to be someone who would kidnap me and cut me up into small pieces.

After I reviewed his paperwork (which took considerable effort on his part to locate), I got into the backseat.

As we pulled away from the curb, he picked up his phone and his radio handset and talked to someone (maybe back in the office?). His voice was low.

He didn't realize that I am fluent in Spanish, as it was the language I learned after English.

This is what he said:

"At first I think I'm picking up some kind of little person going to the airport—because she has luggage. But then I get closer, and I see it's just a girl. I'm telling you, man, it's some kind of undercover sting operation. She asked for all my paperwork! I would have stepped on the gas and sped off, but she was leaning in through the window. This is harsh, my friend. If a kid can ambush you outside of a middle school, what's next?"

Two things.

I had never been in a taxi before.

And I had never ridden in a car with a complete stranger.

I was suddenly an explorer and a risk-taker.

I could feel my heart pounding. It felt good. A smile spread across my face.

I was on my way to see a new friend.

Granted, the person in question was two years older than me, and looked to have some anger management issues (as well as a brother who had discipline and authority problems).

But no living thing is perfect.

All scientists know that.

When we arrived at the school district administration parking lot, and I had paid the negotiated fare, with the addition of an eighteen percent tip, I felt very pleased because I had done this all myself.

I looked Jairo Hernandez right in the eye and said:

"Never let someone tell you that you can't do it."

And then I shut the car door.

I was speaking about my own achievement, but from the look on his face, I think he believed that I was talking about him.

As I came around the corner, I saw Mai sitting on the top stair outside the entrance to Dell's office.

Maybe I was imagining this, but I thought the teenaged girl looked happy to see me.

I quickened my pace while still maintaining control of

my red case with the 360-degree spinning wheel option.

When I got to the trailer, I was able to say what I had been waiting all week to spring on her:

"Chị có khoẻ không?"

She said my greeting had perfect inflection.

I had learned eighty-five Vietnamese phrases over the last seven days, as well as a great deal of verb conjugation.

Now I tried some more of them out on her.

Mai was incredibly impressed—not just that I could say these things, but also because she spent two weeks trying to teach a friend's mother four words of Vietnamese and had not succeeded.

So this effort was worthy.

The time flew by.

We conversed, at first in English and then in bits of Vietnamese.

I usually found so-called "small talk" boring.

I like "large talk," which is more about theories and concepts, mixed with facts and known quantities.

But we didn't have any problem finding things to say to each other, because right away Mai wanted to know about the garden behind my house.

All that greenery had intrigued her.

I told her about some of my plants and gave a simple explanation of a few of my backyard botanical experiments.

And then the next thing I knew, forty minutes had passed and the trailer door opened and Dell Duke appeared with Quang-ha at his side.

The counselor's eyes widened at the sight of us together.

He wanted to know how long I'd been out there and what we'd been talking about.

Dell Duke was not as friendly as I would have thought. And I got the idea that maybe he wanted to push the Nguyen siblings right down the stairs.

His smile was stiff and awkward as he said:

"All right then. It's time for Willow's session. Good-bye, kids."

I insisted on keeping the door to the trailer open so that I could watch as Mai and Quang-ha receded into the distance.

At the last moment, just before the pair turned the corner to head down the block, Mai looked back and waved toward the trailer.

The door was angled, so I felt certain that Mai couldn't see me.

But she knew that I was there.

Suddenly I had a strange lump in my throat.

I had a new, older friend. A girl from high school.

She felt like a protector.

It was some kind of magic.

I settled into the chair and listened to Dell Duke.

Today I wasn't going to take tests.

He said that we were going back to word games.

This time, he would say an industry, and I would say "long-term" or "short-term" projected financial growth.

I explained to him before we started that I had very little knowledge of economics.

I really considered this study a social science, not a hard science, and I wasn't interested in the squishy stuff, so I had stayed away.

But he didn't listen.

He was prepared for our session and had a clipboard covered with scrawled notes.

I could read upside-down pretty easily and I saw right away that he lacked organization of any kind.

His lists had stuff crossed out and then arrows and all sorts of redirection to bubbles of messy thought.

I decided to ignore it.

The first thing he said was:

"Pharmaceutical companies."

Dell had instructed me to answer "high growth," "medium growth," "no growth," or "eroding market."

This was a really crummy game.

I thought that pharmaceutical companies were probably always growing because more medications were constantly being developed; and the field of medicine was so rapidly advancing.

That was just a fact.

So the answer would have to be "high growth," especially with an aging population.

But I said "eroding market" because I decided that I wanted to play the opposite game.

I just didn't tell him.

I was going to see if he was paying attention.

But what was sad was that he never caught on and shouted "You're playing the opposite game."

He just kept writing down my junk.

On my way home I evaluated my situation.

Being a Sequoia Giant had been a colossal disappointment.

But going to the new school led to seeing the round-headed counselor, and that enabled me to meet my new friend, Mai.

School was better since I figured out that all I had to

do to get out of P.E. (and the violent sport of volleyball) was say I had a migraine headache.

I claimed that I was going blind from the pain, and I then got sent to lie down in the nurse's office.

I knew that the nurse, Miss Judi, liked me because we discussed things like flu outbreaks and the statistics behind spontaneous nosebleeds.

So by the time I walked back up Citrus Court to the front door of our house, I was very happy.

chapter 13

jairo hernandez

A pilgrim is a traveler going to a spiritual place.

❧

J airo looked over at the paperwork on the seat next
to him. His license. His vehicle inspection information.

When he started driving a cab, it was only supposed to
be a temporary job.

And now years had passed.

Jairo picked up his radio and told the office that he was
going on break.

He then drove straight to Bakersfield College, where
he picked up a brochure for the Career Pathway program,
which was a continuing education opportunity for people
over the age of thirty.

He was going to investigate the requirements to be a
medical technician.

The girl he picked up that afternoon had rattled his
mobile cage.

He realized that she was some kind of shaman when
she said:

"Never let someone tell you that you can't do it."

She was a blinking warning light.

And Jairo paid attention to signs.

For the first time in his career, Dell thought about his work when he went home that day.

Fate had delivered Alberta Einstein into his life and he had to figure out a way to take advantage of that.

Maybe she could make him smarter?

It certainly appeared as if she could improve his financial situation.

One thing was for certain: With her in his life, everything was happening so fast!

Chapter 14

T he next week I went online and ordered a cab from Mexicano Taxi again. In the special comments/requests box I asked for Jairo Hernandez.

He was on time and had his license and vehicle inspection records ready for me on the front seat.

I checked them again because I think it's important to always be thorough.

As Jairo pulled away from the curb, I noticed two things.

The first was that he had just gotten a haircut. The second reveal was more alarming.

Because his hair was shorter in the back, I could now see a nevus on his neck.

This means I saw a mole.

But not a regular-looking mole. It had, in my opinion, the signs of trouble: It was asymmetrical and it had flecks of red and blue on the broken edges.

One infant in one hundred babies is born with moles. I doubt that's fun for the parents.

Who wants a spotty kid?

But almost all moles appear in the first twenty years of a person's life.

And that is why if a new mole appears, or an old one changes into something else, attention needs to be directed to this area (medically speaking).

I didn't want to alarm Jairo Hernandez.

But there was a real possibility that he might not be aware of this bad-looking mole, because it was on the back of his neck and he couldn't see there very easily.

So while we drove across town to my appointment with Mr. Dell Duke, I stared at his skin issue.

And I felt compelled to write the following on an index card:

> You need to have a dermatologist perform a punch biopsy on the mole (nevus) on the back of your neck. If it is not too much of an invasion of your privacy, I would very much like to look at the pathology report. I will be taking a taxi next week at this same time. This is important, so please do not take this medical suggestion lightly.
>
>   Willow Chance

I handed him the message when I got out of the taxi.

Mai and I were able to talk more easily now in Vietnamese.

I had effectively mastered the tones and accent by obsessive listening at night to audio lessons designed for state department employees.

You could download the sessions if you had a password, which was not hard to get if you knew what you were doing.

It was like we had a secret language, because on the school property no one else but Quang-ha spoke Vietnamese.

We walked around the buildings and the parking lot, still half looking for Cheddar, but really just talking.

We were both interested in botany, and I tried to explain some of the things I knew without sounding like the host of the Discovery Channel.

We were sitting under one of the few trees out in front of the main school district office when I said to her, in Vietnamese:

"You are my new best friend."

Mai was silent. I knew that she had many friends at school, and that her friend Alana was the one she considered to be her closest friend.

I was just a little kid, and I realized that I had overstepped.

What kind of person only knew someone for a few weeks and said something like that?

So I added:

"Since I just started at a new school, you're right now sort of my only friend, so that makes the distinction perhaps not much of a difference."

And that made Mai smile.

chapter 15

roberta & jimmy chance

In American Sign Language, the motion for the word parents is to follow mom with the sign for dad.

〜

Roberta Chance was finally at her doctor's appointment.

It had been over a year since she'd first seen a small dimple on the left side of her chest.

She was going to bring up the little dent during the exam, but Dr. Pedlar saw it before she even had a chance.

The next thing Roberta knew, she was being sent to the Bakersfield Imaging Center just down the street.

They wouldn't even consider making an appointment for the future.

They wanted her over there now.

It was only three blocks away, so Roberta left her car and walked over.

The medical technician at the imaging center seemed to know that she was coming, but the woman didn't smile when she handed her the lavender smock.

And most everyone smiled at Roberta because she had that way about her.

It wasn't until she put back on her street clothes after the ultrasound that it occurred to her something was wrong. That was when the doctor asked her to come to his office.

Because wasn't she already in his office?

Did he mean someplace where he did bookkeeping or ate take-out food for lunch?

Roberta followed Dr. Trocino down the narrow hallway and into a small room with framed pictures of pink angels.

On the doctor's desk was a vase filled with silk flowers that might have once looked good, but now were dusty and faded on the side that faced the window.

It was there, sitting in an upholstered chair that felt moist, like someone might have peed in it and the whole thing never dried right, that the doctor told her the news.

Her dent was a tumor.

The physician's mouth was moving and she could hear what he was saying, but it didn't mean anything because this wasn't happening to her.

Someone else was in the chair.

And then the doctor stood up and said he'd give her a moment to herself and that she should call her husband.

Jimmy Chance operated heavy equipment, which is how he and Roberta had met.

Just out of high school, they'd both signed up for an introductory class to get a commercial driver's license.

Roberta was the only girl taking the course, but Jimmy would have noticed her even if the room had been full of beauties, because she was open and confident.

But he was really attracted to her because Roberta was happy and that showed.

Now, as he left work to meet her at the medical center, he felt like he was the sick one.

What did it all mean? They said that the surgery needed to be scheduled immediately. Her voice was so dull on the phone.

The only other time he'd heard Roberta sound that way was when the man in the fertility clinic had said they couldn't have children.

It had taken his wife all of ten minutes to decide that they would adopt, and her enthusiasm for life then immediately returned.

That took four years to happen, but the adoption had worked out. So this would work out. There would be an answer. There had to be. For him. For Willow. For her.

Yes. For her.

Because he would do anything . . .

For her.

Roberta and Jimmy sat outside the medical center on a wooden bench that was dirty.

She put her shoulder blades back and realized that she was leaning against crusty bird droppings.

Did birds get cancer?

Jimmy was holding her hand but they were both silent. She was glad for that.

There was so much to say but really so little. They had long ago said what mattered to each other.

Roberta put her head on his shoulder and sitting there, in silence, she didn't think about herself. Or about her husband. She thought about Willow.

Her love for her daughter now literally made it hard to breathe.

Roberta shut her eyes to keep the tears trapped under her eyelids. She made her decision.

They wouldn't tell her. Willow was far too interested in medicine to deal with this right now.

They would let her in on the situation when it was over.

After what seemed like five minutes, but was actually over an hour, they got up to go.

They decided to leave Roberta's car in the parking lot

down the street and take Jimmy's pickup truck so that they could be together as they drove across town to the next appointment.

They would not be alone now until this thing was figured out.

Ever.

It was mid-afternoon and the sun beat down in a brutal way. Drivers were cranky as they navigated through congested streets, not giving an inch. It was every car for himself. Or herself.

But Jimmy and Roberta were in their own world in the front seat of the pickup. They were traveling down Eye Street and up ahead the traffic light was red.

Jimmy slowed, but before he came to a full stop the light changed to green.

Ordinarily he would have looked to see if anyone was entering the intersection.

But not today.

Not now.

Jimmy's hand reached over and touched his wife's arm and at the exact moment that he made this connection, the world literally came apart.

They were T-boned in the middle of the intersection by a driver for Med-Service Hospital Supplies. His box truck was loaded down with oxygen tanks and he was already forty minutes behind schedule.

The driver watched the traffic light turn to yellow and then he stepped on the accelerator believing he could just glide right through the red signal.

Instead, he sailed straight into a pickup truck.

Jimmy died on the scene but was still put into an ambulance and taken to the hospital with his wife.

Roberta stopped breathing three hours later during emergency surgery.

The driver was left in a coma.

The only piece of metal not mangled or burned by the collision was a yellow triangle with black lettering on the back bumper, which read:

SAFETY FIRST! Tell Me How I'm Doing:
Call 800 Med-Supp. I'm truck #807.

chapter 16

M ai and I sat outside today on the steps of the
trailer office.

When the door swung open, and Dell and Quang-ha
emerged, I got to my feet and followed Mai down the
stairs.

Dell's forehead crunched up.

"What are you doing?"

Mai gave Dell a sly smile.

"Willow doesn't want to have a session today. But
we were thinking maybe we would all go for ice cream.
Chocolate-dipped cones would be nice."

Dell looked like he had just lost bowel control. He
stammered:

"Willow h-has an appointment. That's not something
th-that's optional."

I glanced off into the distance. Quang-ha couldn't hold
back a snicker.

Dell turned from Mai to me.

"Willow, you've been ordered to come here for behavioral reasons. It's not optional."

I looked right at him.

"I was sent here under false pretense."

For the first time Quang-ha actually seemed interested in what was going on. He said:

"Why does she have to be counseled? She hangs out with my kid sister, so she can't be any kind of trouble-maker."

Dell appeared panicked. He started to babble:

"You—I . . . We must . . . this to-day—"

Mai came to the rescue. She stared at the counselor (whose arms were now giving a strange flap as if he were trying to fly) and said:

"We wanna go to Fosters Freeze. You could drive us. You and Willow can talk about her counseling in the car."

I could see on Dell's face that he was shocked at how cheeky the teenager was.

Then Mai spoke to me in Vietnamese and I answered her. She said that she thought our plan was working. I told her that I agreed.

Dell and Quang-ha both looked surprised. I guess they were unprepared for us to share the language.

The next thing we knew, we were all in Dell Duke's dusty car, heading out of the parking lot to Fosters Freeze.

And that's where it all began, really.

Because as I watched the school district offices recede into the distance, I was certain that the old dynamic between Dell and Mai and me was over.

And endings are always the beginnings of something else.

chapter 17

back in the now

⟨๑⟩

N ext of kin.
That's what they want to know. Kinfolk. Who talks like that?

But that's what they are asking me.

One of the kinfolk is in the Valiant Village, which is a care facility for patients suffering from dementia.

This "kin" is my father's mom.

My grandma Grace sits in a chair in the lobby in front of a non-working fireplace. She even takes her meals on a tray there.

An aid feeds her.

G.G.'s husband died of a heart attack on his sixty-sixth birthday and she started to lose track of things after that.

Should I tell them?

My dad had one brother, but he was older and drifted away from the family when he found work overseas doing private contracting for the military.

No one had heard from him in years; my dad didn't even know if his own brother was still alive.

I tried to find him when I was ten years old, and

from what I pieced together, I'm pretty certain that he died in some kind of accident involving a cargo plane.

But I didn't tell my parents.

And my mom was an only child. Both of her parents passed away when she was in her late twenties. I never even got to meet them.

I don't have aunts and uncles and cousins. We aren't that kind of family. We've had misfortune and a lot of bad health. And now this.

Thinking about the kinfolk health histories was the only time I found comfort in being adopted.

Now I cannot think.

I cannot concentrate.

I cannot breathe.

No.

No.

No.

No.

No.

No.

No.

After a lot of questions, all that I say to the officers is: "I have one grandma who thinks every day is Tuesday."

The shadows get longer.

I sit on the front steps.

The tears will not stop.

And I almost never cry.

But I'm not myself.

I will forever be someone else now.

The two people I need to get in touch with, the two people who most need to hear this most horrible news, are not here.

My teeth start to chatter.

I want to shut my eyes and make everything stop.

I no longer care if my heart pounds in my chest or if my lungs move.

Who are they even moving for?

Mai sits next to me, and her hand grips my shoulder.

She makes a low cooing noise. It is a drawn-out call like a dove makes. And it comes from somewhere deep inside.

I try to focus everything on this sound.

It makes me think, for just an instant, of the tiny squeak that the little green-rumped parrot baby made when he fell from the nest in our backyard years ago.

I look over at her and see that Mai is crying too.

The police officers, with Dell Duke at their jutting elbows, make phone calls. To the police station. To Social Services. To a dozen different workers and agencies as they look for someone who will tell them what to do.

I don't listen.

But I hear them.

I cannot count anymore by 7s.

I hear a voice in my head and it says "Make this stop."

That's all I know.

Should they take me into something called "protective custody"?

If they can't locate next of kin, can they turn me over to a family friend?

I have to go to the bathroom, and finally, that feeling is overwhelming.

I take out my house key and give it to Mai, who opens the door.

When I step inside, I feel certain that my mother will be in the kitchen.

My father will be coming around the corner from the garage and he will be wearing my mom's Peeper glasses.

This has all been a big mistake.

But the house is dark and no one is there.

It is a house now of only ghosts.

It is only a museum of the past.

We

are

d o n e.

chapter 18

～

Willow was finally willing to go inside, to use the bathroom.

Mai gave her a cold, wet towel to hold to her face.

The teenage girl then found a paper grocery bag in a drawer in the kitchen. She went down the hall to Willow's room, where she stood for a moment in the door frame and stared.

It didn't look like where a twelve-year-old kid would live.

All the walls had floor-to-ceiling bookshelves and they were full. There were more things to read in this room than in some bookstores.

Just above the desk (which had a microscope and an elaborate computer setup) was a bulletin board covered with photographs of plants.

Mai moved to the bed, where red pajamas were folded neatly on an espresso-colored comforter. She stuffed them into the paper bag. Mai turned to leave and that's when she noticed the top book on the tall stack of reading material sitting on Willow's night table.

It was open and face-down.

From the position of the spine, Mai could tell that it was almost finished.

She moved closer and she saw that the book was from the Bakersfield public library and it was called *Understanding Vietnamese Customs and Traditions*.

And that was when Mai knew that Willow was coming with her.

She lied.

She told the police that she'd known Willow for many years, not for only weeks.

She said that her mother would sign any paperwork because the families were very, very close.

Dell Duke didn't contradict her because Mai was so convincing that he now half believed her story.

Quang-ha, unnerved by the police, had stayed the whole time in Dell's car. He hadn't moved a muscle.

So Mai was taken as the authority on the situation.

As Dell pulled his car away, he could see neighbors coming out onto the sidewalk. But Willow, with her eyes closed in the backseat, saw nothing.

Dell drove as slowly as he'd ever maneuvered a vehicle, heading across town to the nail salon with the patrol car behind him.

No one knew it, but they passed through the very intersection where Jimmy and Roberta Chance had been hit.

There was still an official vehicle on the scene, but what was left of the pickup and the box truck had been taken away.

There were four gray coils on the pavement where flares had burned out.

Dell's car drove straight over the ash.

They swung into the parking lot in front of Happy Polish Nails, and Mai opened the car door immediately. She and Quang-ha seemed to be in a race to get inside the shop.

But Willow didn't move.

Dell decided to wait with her, but it was killing him.

The real action was obviously going on behind the plate-glass window that had purple sausage-shaped writing, which said:

MAN + PED EURO-STYLE SPECIAL!
WALK-INS VERY WELCOME!

Dell read the message at least a dozen times and could make no sense of it.

He had to concentrate.

Not only were two people dead, but there would now be all kinds of official reports filed, and it was going to become pretty darn obvious that Mr. Dell Duke had taken three kids from the school district off school property to have ice cream and French fries and look at geese.

Talk about terrible timing.

There were police involved and social workers already on high alert.

This was a nightmare.

In so many ways.

It was crucial that Dell look professional, which was one of the hardest things for him to do.

He glanced up into the rearview mirror at Willow.

She had her eyes closed, yet tears still oozed out of the corners and ran at intervals down her dark cheeks.

He wished that he could think of something to say that would be comforting to her. He was, after all, a trained counselor.

And so he turned to the backseat and sputtered:

"This is such a big loss."

He then exhaled and more words dribbled out like applesauce from a baby's mouth. Just audible lumps:

"It's not much consolation, but you'll probably never have any loss this big again."

Dell continued, unable to stop himself.

"So that's kind of comforting—knowing that the worst thing in life is already behind you. I mean, once it actually *is* behind you. Which it won't be for a while, obviously."

To Dell's horror, her level of distress seemed to increase with his every word.

What was he talking about?

Dell cleared his throat and tried to steady his voice as he finished with:

"Because this is life. And these things just happen . . ."

Wow. Did he really just say that?

How many kids go to school and come home to find that both of their parents are dead? Maybe in war-torn Somalia or someplace like that. Then maybe he could legitimately say: "These things happen."

But here?

In Bakersfield?

A total meatball move.

Dell bit down on the inside of his left cheek and held his mouth closed until he could detect the taste of blood.

That's what it took to shut himself up.

chapter 19

pattie nguyen

A leader organizes people whether they know it or not.

⌐๑⌐

I t was a slow afternoon at the salon and Pattie was doing inventory, which was never her favorite thing.

But it had to be done. Bottles of nail polish vanished almost every day. She was certain that it was the result of theft from both her workers and her clients, so it was essential to stay on top of the situation.

As a small-business owner, you had to show that you cared about these things, even if the nail polish, bought in bulk, only ended up costing her sixty-nine cents a pop.

That was one of the secrets to success: caring about the big things *and* the small things.

Or in Pattie's case, you cared about everything.

She wished all of her customers just wanted red nails. Red was lucky.

But Pattie carried over one hundred shades in their squat little glass containers.

She put down a bottle of fire-engine red and picked

up peacock blue, a new shade that was very popular but carried no good fortune.

With the annoying blue in her right hand, she looked through the front window and suddenly saw a dusty sedan pull into the parking lot.

A police car was right behind it.

Not good.

Maybe if she had kept the red bottle in her hand, this wouldn't have happened. She knew that wasn't logical, but still.

And then she watched, her heart rate increasing, as her two kids got out of the dirty Ford and rushed toward the salon.

Really not good.

Pattie dropped the little glass bottle straight into the trash. She was going to discontinue carrying the unlucky peacock-blue nail polish.

In the very first week of school, Quang-ha had cut classes and gotten into arguments with teachers. He was in danger of being expelled.

Pattie had asked the principal for counseling. She firmly believed that her son needed a voice of authority to scare him back onto the right path.

But not real authority!

Certainly not the police.

And then before she could make a guess at what he'd done, her kids were inside the salon and they were both talking at once.

Quang-ha wanted his mother to know that Mai had lied.

This was suddenly an important moment for him because the playing field was being leveled.

Now he wasn't the only one who twisted words to the people in charge.

But Mai, speaking rapid-fire in Vietnamese, raised her voice above his.

This wasn't about lying.

This was about a car accident and a girl who had lost her parents. Mai only cared about that.

Quang-ha argued that they didn't even know the little kid. Getting involved on any level was trouble.

Pattie tried to sort it out but it wasn't long until both of the police officers were standing in front of her getting ready to launch an avalanche of questions in her direction.

Before they could, Mai took her mother's hand and pulled her toward the door. Pattie followed, moving right past the two cops.

Mai led her straight to Dell's car, where she wordlessly opened the backseat door so that her mother could be face-to-face with Willow.

Pattie saw grief.

Her eyes focused on a version of her own young self, and so many other children in Vietnam who grew up without parents, some abandoned because of their ethnicity, others because of tragedy.

And her arms reached out wide.

⌒⌒

After Pattie signed the bottom of the paperwork that gave her legal responsibility for Willow for the next twenty-four hours, the police cruiser charged out of the parking lot like a getaway car.

That left Dell Duke.

He wanted to be invited home with them. He was now really part of this.

But Pattie ignored him as she went about closing the nail salon early, barking orders in Vietnamese to the two manicurists.

Dell hung around the cash register trying to be relevant.

It wasn't working.

Even though Pattie stood barely over five feet tall to his five foot eight inches, she kept edging him toward the door.

"We talk tomorrow."

She said this more than once, and then suddenly she had a hold of his right elbow as she literally led him outside.

Dell managed to say:

"I should probably get your home number. I mean, I have it in Quang-ha's files at the office, but I . . ."

Pattie either wasn't listening or wasn't interested.

She pulled out a large ring of keys, and with Dell now on the sidewalk, she went back into the salon and began locking the heavy door at the bottom.

Dell was on the wrong side of the thick plate glass. But he continued as if he were still in the room, raising his voice as he said:

"Okay then. I should be going. Which I'll do. Right now. Long day. For all of us . . ."

He strained to get a better look at Willow, but she was crouched down with Mai at her side.

He hadn't even said good-bye.

Pattie then snapped off the bright fluorescent ballasts. The windows were tinted, making it hard to see much of anything inside.

Dell walked to his car. When he glanced over his shoulder the salon was just shadows. They had to be leaving out a back door to go home.

He thought about following their car as they drove away, but suddenly the weight of what had happened, the enormity of the situation, hit him hard.

Dell got into his Ford, slid the key into the ignition, and then burst into tears.

His neck muscles seemed to give way, and as he sobbed, his head fell forward and hit the steering wheel.

And that's when the horn sounded, startling him and the world around him into a new consciousness.

chapter 20

I've never seen this person in my life.

But her arms are around me.

Tight.

Because the woman is so strong, you'd think her hug would choke me.

But instead, it's the first time I can get a full breath into my lungs since I heard what happened.

They live behind the nail salon in a garage.

A real garage, not one converted to anything. You could move things and still drive a car in here.

There is no bathroom.

They walk across the alley back to the salon, where there is a toilet and a tiny shower stall made of molded plastic.

They don't think living in the garage is weird.

Because they are used to it.

The garage has only one window and that looks like it wasn't part of the original construction.

I'm certain someone just cut out a square in the un-insulated stucco-on-plywood wall.

There is an ancient-looking air conditioner hanging on to the ledge of the bootlegged window, and the glass above the machine has been covered with a piece of decorative cloth.

The fabric has completely faded on the side exposed to the sunlight, and whatever pattern was there is gone. Scorched away.

Despite the air conditioner, it is still incredibly hot in the garage.

Even with the machine on the highest setting.

Mats cover the cracked concrete floor, making a crazy quilt of colored rattan and woven plastic.

There is a queen-size mattress and a single cot pushed together at one end of the garage. That is the sleeping area.

The other space is taken up by a long metal table where two hot plates and a microwave can be seen next to cans of bamboo shoots and water chestnuts.

An assortment of pots and pans hang from hooks on the wooden studs next to ladles and strainers and big boxes of breakfast cereal, which must come from Costco.

Mom buys those.

And just that fact makes my heart beat in a messed-up way.

A small refrigerator is plugged into an adapter that has six different electrical devices all feeding into one outlet.

I know for a fact that's not safe.

And then my thoughts shift.

It might be a good thing if the garage caught on fire.

If I were alone in here.

Because if I got trapped in a blaze started by arcing electrical overload in the wall of the garage, the searing pain of losing my mom and dad would go up in smoke with me.

I would be released then.

I would be set free.

Mai wants to know if I want to lie down.

But I can't speak.

In any language.

Pattie makes soup that is cloudy white with curly pieces of green onion floating on top.

And then there is suddenly a plate with salty pork strips, which appear from nowhere.

Dysphagia is the medical term for not being able to

swallow, and I know that there are two kinds of dysphagia: oropharyngeal and esophageal.

But maybe there is also a third kind of dysphagia that
comes when your heart breaks into pieces.

I can't swallow because I have that kind.

Mai tells her brother to go across the alley.

He only snarls at her.

He asks in Vietnamese:

*"Why are you always telling me what to do? It's just not
right."*

He takes his sweet time, but finally leaves.

Once Quang-ha is gone, Pattie and Mai help me out of
my shoes and baggy pants.

They put me into my red pajamas. I don't know how
the clothes got here.

I still can't eat any of the food.

And not just because I'm a vegetarian.

Mai's mother pours some of the soup into a coffee mug
and she holds it to my lips.

It's like coaxing a baby bird. Little tiny gulps.

I know how hard that is because I was a parrot-parent.

And so I take small sips that taste salty, like drinking
someone's cloudy tears.

And then Pattie lights incense that is in the shape of a triangle and she places it on a red plate.

She bows her head as her eyes glisten and she takes my hand and we both cry.

Mai leans against her mother, and for the first time in my life, my memory disappears.

I know I will remember nothing of this night because I will try as hard as I can to never think of it again.

I will win that battle.

chapter 21

Quang-ha was mad.

That was normal. But this fresh anger struck a deeper chord than most of his sudden bursts of frustration.

Because he already had no privacy.

He slept wedged next to his sister and his mother. What difference did it make that he was on his own mattress?

Who was anyone kidding?

They lived in one room and that was a garage and now they were letting someone view their situation and, even worse, be part of it?

It was all just too much.

The little girl was strange. Couldn't everyone see that?

Look at her clothes and her hair and her glasses and her luggage with the wheels. Listen to her whispery voice and her laugh, which was like someone choking.

Come on—she spoke Vietnamese! What was *that* all about?

Maybe she was some kind of spy or at the very least a complete nerd. You'd only learn the language if it was jammed down your throat—like everything else in his life.

He was not going to feel sorry for her because her parents died in a car crash.

Okay, maybe he felt sorry for her when he first heard, and she was shaking, but he wasn't going to right now.

No way.

No how.

He was going to feel sorry for himself.

Because he didn't ask to be born. He didn't ask to have his father drive off in a truck and never return.

He didn't ask to have every single thing in his life smell like fingernail polish. His clothes and even his shoes had that chemical stink.

And another thing to be mad about was that he slept in his underwear.

How was he supposed to do that now?

The underwear had robots on them. Like a little kid would wear. And he was in high school!

His mother never seemed to know the difference between something cool and something for idiots, because all she cared about was that it was something on sale.

Well, now he'd have to sleep in his pants because he wasn't letting the girl see the robots.

And he hated that, because the pants twisted up around his legs and made it next to impossible to even bend his knees and sleep on his side, which was the most comfortable way.

As if it wasn't already bad enough on the floor of a garage on the wrong side of the tracks in Bakersfield.

∽

The next morning Willow told Mai that she wasn't going to school. She didn't say "ever again," but Mai thought that's how it sounded.

She was pretty definitive.

Quang-ha took a stab at refusing to get a high school education as well, but it didn't work.

And so Quang-ha and Mai gathered up their things and walked down the already hot alley. Mai promised Willow that she'd hurry home the second she got out.

Pattie had been given a telephone number for the Kern County Department of Children's Services. She was supposed to call first thing because Willow was going to be assigned a social worker and officially have her case file opened.

Pattie assumed that relatives would fly into town or that family friends would, once alerted, take over.

Everyone has a network of people in their lives.

Pattie only hoped that the group assembled to care for the odd little girl with the dark, wet eyes would do a good job.

chapter 22

want to turn off the sun and live in darkness.

I wake up on top of a mattress resting on the floor of the garage across the alley from Mai's mom's nail salon.

And I have no idea, for what feels like a very long time, where I am.

I hope that I'm dreaming.

I am not.

Yesterday happened.

The heavy weight of it presses down on me in a force much greater than gravity.

It is crushing.

I am twelve years old and already twice without parents.

If you analyze the odds of being given away at birth and then losing another full set of legal guardians 147 months and 7 days later, I'm right on the edge of the graph.

In the one percent of the one percent.

I can still walk and talk and breathe, but there isn't much point.

It's just something my body is doing.

I'm not going back to school.

You don't have to watch many wildlife documentaries to know that the herd doesn't accept the lone straggler.

And with the exception of Margaret Z. Buckle, the herd never accepted me anyway, so I'm not losing much.

When did middle schools eliminate weekly spelling bees? It's the only activity that I would have signed up for.

There is just one person who I will miss now that I'm no longer a Sequoia Giant.

Miss Judi.

The school nurse.

She saw more of me than any other student and we shared a love of germ eradication.

I wish her well.

I'm sitting in the back of the salon next to the storage closet.

I found a furniture pad and rolled it up in such a way as to make a place for myself.

I wanted to stay across the alley in the garage, which

would be good because it is dark back there, but Pattie insisted I be where she can see me.

I wasn't going to argue.

I barely know the woman.

I didn't have my Healthy-Start breakfast, and not because they have never heard of it, but because I'm still having trouble swallowing.

I have a caseworker.

Pattie Nguyen tells me this after she hangs up the phone.

I ask for paper and a pen. Two of the manicurists arrive. I barely notice them.

I decide to write down my thoughts. But not my real ones. I cannot put on paper the idea that I want to scream, as loud as I can, until my throat ruptures.

So I make a list.

I try to concentrate on that.

An hour later, a woman comes into the salon.

But she doesn't want a manicure.

She has posture that suggests lower lumbar pain. She probably sits in a chair for too long. And has inadequate abdominal strength.

I'd tell her, but I couldn't care less.

Everyone, I now realize, lives in a world of pain. But I'm certain that mine is greater than hers.

The woman with the bad back talks up front to Pattie.

I have no idea for how long.

I'm done measuring things.

I only hear parts of the conversation.

Although it is about me, it doesn't matter.

Nothing that they say will change the fundamental fact of my life, which is so overwhelming that I cannot give voice to it.

I do hear the woman tell Pattie that she's handled many of "these type of cases."

That doesn't seem accurate.

Because how many twelve-year-old kids in Bakersfield actually lose both parents in one afternoon?

I also hear the woman explain that the Jamison Children's Center was established by Kern County "to provide children who need emergency shelter and protection a safe, warm, and nurturing environment."

That can't be good.

The woman does all the talking, and Pattie doesn't respond.

She doesn't even say "uh-huh," or "I understand."

She is like me.

Silent.

I admire that in a person. The ability to keep your mouth shut is usually a sign of intelligence.

Introspection requires you to think and analyze.

It's hard to do that when you are blabbing away.

Finally Pattie motions to the back, and the next thing I know, the official-looking woman leans over me and says:

"My name is Lenore Cole and I'm here to help you."

I hand her a piece of paper.

She looks surprised, but straightens (with a small grimace, which reinforces my diagnosis of lower back pain) and reads:

1. My parents have no relatives who are appropriate to accept legal responsibility for me.

2. I do not believe that any of my parents' small circle of friends are in a position to take me into their lives. We did not belong to any church or other organization that might have support groups.

3. I do not wish to ever return for any reason to the house where I lived on Citrus Road. I would like you to call Haruto Ito, the owner of Ito's Garden Services, and tell him that our backyard garden is now his responsibility. He will understand.

4. I would like to have my computer and my printer, which are in my room. There is a large cabinet

with my medical file cards. I will need these. And I would also like all of the blue notebooks, as well as my clothing, the metal box under my bed with my life's savings, the orange towel in the bathroom, my humidifier, and my copy of <u>Atlas of Human Anatomy</u> by Frank H. Netter and Sharon Colacino. Also my TI-89 Titanium-Plus graphing calculator, which is on my desk. Please be careful with it.

5. I would like all of the pictures of my parents put in storage for me for the future.

6. I would like to formally request a forensic autopsy be performed on both my mom and dad. I will need a copy of this report, although I will not be reading it at this time.

7. I would like my DVD of the movie <u>Adaptation</u>. It is in the cabinet under the television in the living room.

8. I will need the pictures and information pinned up to my bulletin board taken down and placed in a large envelope. Please take special care when handling the lemur photo signed by wildlife legends Beverly and Dereck Joubert.

9. I would like a sedative prescribed to help me deal with anxiety. I may need medication at a later date for depression, but I would need to see extensive research on its long-term effects on teenagers. And

I would also like a complex multi-vitamin designed
specifically for juvenile use.

10. I am going to stay for now at Happy Polish Nail
Salon. It is my hope that the Nguyen family will allow
this, and be compensated for taking care of me.

11. I have 7 library books. They will need to be
returned. I have never incurred a late fee. I don't
want to start now.

Respectfully,
Willow Chance

The woman looks stunned by the clarity of the communication.

Or maybe the intense expression on her face is normal.

Either way, it is a relief that she doesn't smile.

For a period of time, immeasurable now that nothing
can be quantified, my caseworker tries in a variety of ways
to convince me to leave with her.

I say nothing.

And I don't move a muscle other than to take shallow,
almost imperceptible breaths.

I know this can be unsettling to people.

I can't count anymore by 7s, but I can conjugate irregular Latin verbs, and I do this while she speaks to me.

Finally, when it is obvious that none of her talking is
working, the woman implies that force is an alternative.

She doesn't say that she's going to drag me to her car by my hair if that's what it takes.

But I get the picture.

And so in the end I have no choice but to go along.

I'm surprised that I have as much trouble as I do saying good-bye to Pattie Nguyen.

She puts her arms around me tight and I wish that she would stay that way.

But of course she can't.

I don't say anything, but I guess the tears running down my cheeks do the talking, because Pattie abruptly turns away and goes to the back of the salon. It is the hardest good-bye I've ever had.

Yesterday at this time, I didn't even know her.

Chapter 23

Jamison Children's Center is the county facility that provides emergency foster care.

Lenore Cole gives me a pamphlet.

I read it, but get the distinct feeling that the place is probably for kids who have parents who hit them or don't feed them real food because they are too busy taking drugs or stealing something.

As we drive up to the building, I put my index and middle fingers on my carotid artery just behind my ear to take my pulse.

I know for a fact that my heart rate is in some kind of danger zone.

We go inside.

They are processing my paperwork.

When I enter, I see that the doors have locks on both sides. They click shut.

There are surveillance cameras in every room.

People are watching.

It is a big mistake for me to be here.

All of a sudden, I have trouble breathing. I can't get air in. And I can't get air out.

I take a seat on a lime-and-purple upholstered couch and struggle to get a grip on my lungs.

Someone's left a copy of the morning edition of the *Bakersfield News Gazette* on the elephant-shaped metal coffee table.

A photograph takes up most of the space above the fold.

The headline reads:

FIERY CAR CRASH CLAIMS TWO LIVES
Third Person in a Coma

Below the caption I see my dad's demolished pickup, in pieces and burned black, conjoined with a mangled medical truck.

And then everything in my field of vision disappears.

I hit my head on the elephant-shaped coffee table when I experienced syncope, or a transient loss of consciousness, more commonly known as passing out.

Yes, I fainted.

And when I did, the sharp edge of the pachyderm's trunk sliced right into my glabella.

Blood suddenly is everywhere because blows to the head bleed profusely.

I'm in and out of consciousness, and the confusion feels good.

Suddenly there are all kinds of announcements being shouted on the P.A. system.

And then I can hear someone say I need stitches since it's a deep cut and it is right between my eyebrows and it will likely scar.

I murmur:

"My glabella . . ."

But the staff doesn't know that the glabella is the name of the space between your eyebrows.

I hear someone whisper:

"She's asking for Bella!"

I shut my eyes again.

So many things in life are distressing.

The brow of the head is formed specifically to guard against these kinds of injuries.

It is bone, and like the bumper of a car, it's designed to take a blow.

So this is a freak accident to faint and then collapse in such a way as to get sliced between the eyes by the surprisingly dangerous trunk of the elephant coffee table.

But I did.

And now there is blood.

My blood.

Hemoglobin is iron-containing protein that makes up 97 percent of every red blood cell's content, when dry.

But when mixed with water, which is how it courses through the human body, it is only about thirty-five percent.

Hemoglobin is what binds the oxygen.

Now that Jimmy and Roberta Chance are gone, what binds me to this world?

They take me to Mercy Hospital because I am a twelve-year-old girl and they don't want me to have facial disfigurement.

At least that's what I hear someone whisper in the hallway.

The nurse at Jamison puts a bandage over the laceration and asks me to hold an icy compress on my wound, which I do.

And then Lenore Cole and I get back in her car and drive together to Mercy Hospital.

Twice she asks if I'm still bleeding, and I'm wondering if she's worried about her upholstery.

It would look pretty messed up to be a social worker and have dried kid blood as a permanent stain in your vehicle.

They didn't request an ambulance because it wasn't

that kind of injury, but I wouldn't have minded riding in one.

At Mercy, I sit in the waiting room of the E.R. and it doesn't take much to realize that this place doesn't have double locks on the doors or surveillance cameras everywhere like at Jamison.

I get nine stitches.

The old me would have asked for 7, because that was my number.

But the doctor puts in nine.

I don't say anything when he tells me.

It now looks like I have a caterpillar between my eyes.

Yet this is not the most important thing that happens after I collapse onto the now-established-as-dangerous elephant coffee table.

Because after I have a drink of water and, for the fourth time, view my medical chart, I ask to use the bathroom.

I tell Lenore Cole that I'll be right back.

And the woman believes me.

I don't go down the hall to the restroom.

Instead, I take an elevator up to the third floor, and then walk to the other wing of the hospital and use the back stairs to get to the cafeteria.

Once I'm there, I ask a grief-stricken woman (I know

the look) wearing a fuzzy green bathrobe and ski boots if I can use her cell phone.

She doesn't say yes, but she doesn't say no.

And after an awkward amount of time where I just stare at her, she hands me her mobile device.

I dial the number for Mexicano Taxi and make a special request for Jairo Hernandez.

I know his taxi license number and give that to the dispatcher. I say I want to be picked up in front of Century 21 Premier Realty on the corner of Truxton and A Street.

That is one block from the hospital.

When I hand the phone back to the woman in the bathrobe, I notice that she has a hospital band on her wrist.

So she's a patient.

Before everything in my life changed, I would have sat down to discuss her condition.

But now I just say in a voice that sounds automated:

"Get some rest. It is critical to recovery."

And I'm gone.

Chapter 24

✎

Jairo was spooked.

This girl was some kind of mystic.

As she'd suggested, he'd been to see a doctor. And the mole on his neck had been removed *that morning*. He was now waiting for the report. The biopsy.

But the doctor had made it clear that the ugly black hunk of skin was something bad.

He hadn't told anyone at work, and he had a scarf around his neck to cover the bandage.

He looked down at his right hand and realized it was shaking.

Jairo shut his eyes and mouthed a prayer. He never did that. But this was serious.

Even a non-believer would believe.

Now, as he pulled up to the curb, he could see that she'd been in some kind of accident, because she had a line of stitches between her eyes, which were both puffy and red.

It looked like she'd been doing a lot of big-time crying.

He wanted to know what happened.

Had someone hurt her?

He felt a wave of anger roll over him. If someone did this girl wrong, they would have *him* to deal with.

The undersized twelve-year-old got into his taxi, and in a whisper of a voice said that she did not have the money to pay for the fare.

She asked if she could get it to him later in the week, or by mail—whatever worked better for his schedule.

Jairo said yes, of course, he would take her anywhere.

No charge.

She wanted to go to Beale Memorial Library.

That was only a few miles away, but it was hot out and she said that she wasn't up to walking anywhere.

Jairo asked if she was okay, and she only nodded and then shut her eyes.

He put on his turn indicator and pulled back out into the lane. He realized that he'd lived in Bakersfield for eleven years and he'd never been inside the library.

That was wrong.

It was for the public and it was filled with knowledge.

Jairo understood as he drove that he needed to stop listening to crazy guys yell at each other on sports radio and start thinking about something that had consequences that were real and important.

She was guiding him.

He knew that now.

Yes.

She was his angel.

As they neared her destination, Jairo glanced into the rearview mirror. The ghost/prophet/inspector/angel was gnawing some kind of plastic strip off her wrist.

A hospital band?

That's what it looked like.

Why was he just now seeing that?

He was going to have to learn to be a better observer of all things.

But most especially of his own life.

When she got out of his taxi, she told him that he would hear from her.

He didn't doubt that.

And then as he watched, she headed into the library.

In the backseat there was a small trash bag. Jairo reached inside and pulled out the plastic hospital scrap.

On the band was written:

Willow Chance I.D. number 080758-7

He would play those numbers at Lotto for the rest of his life.

Chapter 25

Yes, he worked for the Bakersfield Unified School System. And, well, ah, yes, he'd heard—or rather—he *knew* that there had been an accident involving the parents of one of the children he was helping.

He had to concentrate. To focus. Fear had a way of scrambling his brain.

What was the woman going on about?

"The police report said that you brought her home . . ."

Dell was grinding his teeth as his jaw slid back and forth and his tongue sucked up into the roof of his mouth, forming a kind of foamy vacuum.

He was able to break it long enough to say:

"Yes, I'd been working with her. I'm a counselor. It's just a tragedy."

And then he heard:

"We'd like you to come down to Jamison. You could be part of the search."

It was like the sun suddenly poked through a stormy sky. Everything changed color and tone and intensity.

"The search . . . ?"

The voice now replied:

"She's missing. You could be helpful."

There might even have been bells somewhere far away now ringing.

Dell found his voice rising two octaves.

"I *could?*"

Dell left work, driving ten blocks out of his way to pass the Chance house, where several dozen bouquets of flowers from neighbors and coworkers lay wilted from the heat on the front steps.

Someone had made a homemade banner that said:

JIMMY AND ROBERTA R.I.P.

But the evening wind from the night before must have gotten hold of the sign, because now it was on the neighbor's dry front lawn.

A group of burned-low votive candles sat on the walkway and a half-dozen empty beer bottles were on their sides nearby.

It looked, Dell thought, like the remains of a bad party.

Willow Chance, according to the assembled authorities—was he part of them now? It looked like it!—had no viable relatives.

But now the kid was missing.

They had sent a patrol car to Happy Polish and she wasn't there.

The woman in charge was playing a version of the blame game, accusing all kinds of people of being at fault.

He knew that game well, having been a finger-pointer since early childhood.

When in doubt, pout. Or falsely accuse someone.

But one thing in the muddle of confusion was clear: He was being asked to help.

He could sense his power in the room. It was a new feeling and it made him literally dizzy.

What if he could actually find the missing kid?

They were focusing on "foul play." Abductors who might have been caught on video cameras or other means of surveillance.

But Dell knew in his heart that the twelve-year-old hadn't met with any kind of foul play.

It was more likely that she was assisting a doctor performing open-heart surgery than that some creep had snatched her.

But he didn't show his hand.

And so while Lenore huddled with other employees filing police reports and requesting interviews with hospital workers, Dell excused himself and accessed the school district website.

He then drove straight to Mai's high school.

Chapter 26

I would live here at Beale Memorial Library, if it were any kind of viable option.

But it's not like the classic book where the two kids run away from home and go to hide in a museum in New York City.

I know that I need a bed, and I like to take frequent baths and showers. Brushing my teeth is very important and not just because of the proven connection between poor oral hygiene and heart attacks.

But as I walk through the double doors of this place I do wish that it were possible. Because:

$$books = comfort$$

To me anyway.

And comfort is a thing of the past.

I have trouble concentrating, but I still attempt to search for reading material involving losing a parent.

I find no literature or empirical data directed to a middle schooler.

If I were a publisher, I would immediately initiate a

series of books for kids who have to cope with the death of their mother or father.

And I would include an entire edition for those who have lost both of their parents at the same time.

But despite my own situation, I do not believe that there is a large enough need for useful information about losing two parents twice.

I find an abandoned piece of paper on a desk, and after borrowing a pen at the front counter, I write:

> There must be commonality in the experience of losing a parent that makes it worthwhile to share the particulars of the occurrence.
>
> Especially for the young.
>
> More literary output is needed from professionals in this area.
>
> Please pass along this request to the appropriate people in the world of publishing.

I then fold the paper in half and slip it into the suggestion box, which is located next to the water fountain on the first floor.

And then I head up to the second level.

You are not allowed to sleep in the library.

I know this because I've seen the security guard wake people.

It's a rule to keep the homeless from taking over the place.

I feel overwhelming empathy for that group right now.

We are one.

But I know this building.

And upstairs, in the far corner, are big molded chairs that look like doughnuts.

I crawl behind a red one.

I tuck my knees up against my chest and only my shoes stick out.

Camouflage is a form of crypsis, which means hiding.

The skin on my ankles is dark and I'm wearing a pair of brown work boots.

The carpeting in here is also shades of tan and chocolate. It is a pattern of swirls and dots, no doubt installed to camouflage any dirt.

I'm hiding in plain sight, which is often the best way to be concealed.

And in only seconds, I'm asleep.

chapter 27

Dell went to the front office and made a request to speak with Mai Nguyen.

He showed his credentials and, though a few eyebrows were raised, only minutes later the scrappy fourteen-year-old was escorted out of class and stood in front of him.

Mai's fiery eyes narrowed as they noticed Dell.

What was *he* doing here?

At the same time that she was mildly freaked out by the sight of the bearded counselor, she was also excited. She'd never been plucked out of class before.

All the teenagers had stared as she was led from the stuffy room. Mai wondered if her classmates assumed it had something to do with her shady brother.

She had to admit the thought had crossed her own mind.

But no. Mr. Duke wanted to see *her*.

It wasn't until the nosy receptionist had finally left them alone in the cramped little room (which smelled like the sweat-soaked stuff in the overflowing lost-and-found box) that the counselor got down to business.

He blurted out:

"Willow is missing."

Mai was not one for drama. Her voice was unmoved as she replied:

"What's that supposed to mean?"

Dell felt his jaw clench.

This girl needed an attitude adjustment! She should have been intimidated by him and at the same time shown deep concern for her missing friend.

He saw no evidence of either.

Dell cleared his throat and reminded himself not to get too cranked up.

"A woman from Social Services picked her up from your mother's nail salon. Willow was at their facility when she fell and cut her forehead. She needed stitches and it was all taken care of at the emergency room at Mercy. But then before they could leave she said she had to go to the bathroom and no one's seen her since."

Mai's eyes narrowed.

"What do you mean she fell?"

Dell's eyes widened. Why did she have to question the facts?

He tried to remain in control.

"She fainted."

Mai's voice was smug.

"That's not falling. Falling is an accident. Fainting is a medical thing."

Dell pulled an old piece of beef jerky out of the inside pocket of his jacket and ripped off a chunk with his coffee-stained teeth.

He silently cursed himself for thinking this smart-mouth teenage sister of the troublemaker known as Quang-ha could ever help.

He found himself chewing the jerky with loud, thrashing vigor, hoping it made him look tough, not just hungry.

"Her injury is not the point. Maybe I didn't make myself clear. The problem is that no one can find her."

Mai couldn't help but smile. Willow had given them the slip.

"You took her to the hospital?"

Dell was relieved that he could at least answer:

"No. They only brought me in to help find her after she disappeared."

Mai liked that his idea of finding Willow was to come to her for help. She smiled as she said:

"She will probably end up back at the salon. But I have some ideas for where she'd go before she gets there. You need to sign me out of here."

Dell didn't like the way that sounded. This wasn't an episode of *CSI: Bakersfield*. They weren't all of a sudden crime-fighting partners! He wanted Mai to give him a few leads. That was all.

Dell sputtered:

"Well, I didn't—that wasn't what I—"

But Mai was already out of her chair and heading for the door.

chapter 28

~✦~

My eyes open and I realize that I'm looking at a pair of green shoes without laces.

I know these feet.

One of the shoes lightly taps my left boot for what I realize must be the second time.

But I'm wedged back between the doughnut-chair and the wall, and I have to wiggle out.

When I do, I see my teenage friend, who whispers:

"They're looking for you."

The Old Me would have been flooded with shame or worry or guilt.

But not now.

Mai looks at me more closely.

"You got stitches. How long do they stay in?"

My hand goes up to check my glabella. I forgot about the elephant attack.

I mumble:

"They are made from Vicryl, which is polyglycolic acid. They will absorb by hydrolysis. So I won't have to have them taken out."

Mai appears to understand the principle of absorption. "Do they hurt?"

I'm not able to feel anything between my eyes right now, but my hip is sore from the position on the floor.

And the rest of me is just so emotionally numb that I have no idea where the pain stops and starts. I pull myself into a seated position and my right hand goes up to my cheek.

I have the swirled carpet pattern on one whole side of my face. I must have been asleep for a while.

Mai continues:

"Dell Duke is trying to find you. Maybe there's some kind of reward, because he's pretty fired up."

The smile on Mai's face is both kind and wicked at the same time.

I admire that in her.

Dell calls Social Services right away and I hear him report the news.

He is extremely excited.

I get in his car and sit in the back with Mai like we are in a taxi, which we are not.

Dell thinks that he's going to take me right back to Jamison, but Mai puts her foot down, metaphorically speaking.

She says we must go to someplace called Happy Jack's Pie n' Burger shop.

He doesn't stand a chance against her.

And not just because she says that she's going to open the door and jump out of the moving car if she doesn't get her way.

Mai whispers to me that she's never actually been in the hamburger and pie place, but she's driven by many times and I guess she intuitively believes that a place named "happy" might be moving the car in the right direction.

She says she wants to try their French fries.

Mai is thin, but I'm starting to realize that she has a monster appetite, especially for things that she previously has been denied.

I don't say anything about the long-term health issues associated with potato consumption, which has a link to juvenile weight gain.

I'm done with my job as consumer advocate/health adviser.

Inside Happy Jack's, I sit, puffy-eyed, next to Mai, who orders me a slice of chocolate peanut butter pie.

We are in a booth with a very high back and I can see right away that Mai likes it here.

She says it's cozy.

It takes some effort, but I manage to eventually com- municate that I'd like hot water with honey and three tablespoons of white vinegar. This is harder than it should be.

Dell orders a cup of coffee.

The school counselor goes back and forth between looking very happy and very anxious.

I ignore the mood swings.

I'm ignoring everything, so it's not too hard.

After our food has arrived, Dell gets up and goes to the bathroom. But I see him peek over his shoulder before he disappears behind the squeaky men's room door.

His face says that we're potential runaways.

He doesn't need to worry because I know for a fact that Mai's not leaving this place until she's finished her French fries.

And I've run out of options for fleeing.

But once he's gone, Mai gets up from the table.

I see her talking to our waitress, who is definitely someone's great-grandmother. Or at least old enough to be. She is very kind. I wonder how she'd feel about taking care of a twelve-year-old.

I manage to get down a few small bites of the pie.

Chocolate and peanut butter—despite the fact that I do my best to avoid the intake of refined sugar—are a worthy combination.

But right now the food tastes like a wood product.

Mai comes back, and she and I speak in Vietnamese.

Or to be accurate, Mai speaks in that language. I only listen.

She is still working on her food when Dell returns and flags down the waitress.

He asks for the check and she says:

"You're gonna have to wait for the rest of your order, Big Boy. It's not up yet."

Dell looks at Mai, who is expressionless.

I fixate on the idea of someone calling Dell Duke "Big Boy."

It's a very aggressive thing to do.

Especially if the woman is looking for a good tip.

And then I realize the waitress has him right where she wants him. He looks more anxious now.

But I just stare at my chocolate peanut butter pie with the two missing bites and wonder how it all came to this.

The next step in my journey also turns out to be Mai's idea.

She finds out that Dell's apartment has two bedrooms.

She's talking and I realize that she is giving him an explanation of why her family doesn't have the right kind of living conditions for me.

Dell has no idea about their garage setup. And she's not telling him.

But before Dell realizes what's going on, the teenager is on his cell phone, speaking to her mother in a language that he can't understand.

Minutes later the senior food server returns, carrying a large white sack filled with take-out containers.

Mai gives the waitress a sweet smile and accepts the greasy bag.

Dell looks down at the bill, which has just been dropped in front of him.

In addition to the food on the table, there is a to-go fried chicken dinner, a fish and chips plate, a fresh fruit plate, and six large pickles.

Dell finishes my pie while the waitress runs his credit card.

And he doesn't look happy about it.

Foster parents.

That's what I need.

I have studied astrophysics and even waste management systems in space aircraft, but I have never given any thought to the procedure for custody or guardianship of a minor in the state of California.

Life, I now realize, is just one big trek across a minefield and you never know which step is going to blow you up.

Right now I'm back at Jamison.

They are talking about me in other rooms.

And while it is physically impossible for this to happen, I can hear them.

I've been left in the nurse's office.

No one wants me fainting twice.

The attack elephant was still in place in the waiting area out front. I steered clear of that on my own.

I'm now on an examining bench in a dark room. That white crinkly paper underneath my body means that I literally can't shift a muscle without making the same noise as eating potato chips.

Fortunately, I'm an expert at not moving.

My friends stand outside in the parking lot.

I can see them through the spaces in the window blinds.

From a distance, they look suspicious.

Their bodies are too close and their postures are rigid.

The late-day Bakersfield sun beats down, bouncing off from the cars and the blacktop. Anyone in his or her right mind would have gone inside to the air-conditioned building.

I can see Mai brokering the deal.

She is speaking to her mother. I will find out later that she says:

"We'll put down his address. And then in the future, when they come visit, we can go over and make it look like we live there."

I see that Pattie is silent and her face is sour.

Dell has no idea what's actually happening. Mai talks so fast:

"If we don't do this, they will keep her here. And then they'll just stick her in a foster home. She will end up being put somewhere with people she doesn't even know. She'll run away again!"

Mai stares into her mother's eyes.

"She needs us."

I watch as Pattie breaks the gaze and looks down at Dell's small hands. He chews his fingernails.

I'm guessing that she hates that. She keeps her eyes on his cuticles and I can see her speaking. She is probably saying:

"I don't want to get involved."

It's a strange thing for her to say, because she took a bus over to Jamison as soon as she heard that I had disappeared from the hospital.

If she really didn't want to get involved, what is she doing here?

And then I see Pattie suck in her breath and cross her arms in a way meant to show firm resolve.

I know that posture well.

It was always my mother's last stand.

Decisions are made.

I will officially be turned over to my old family friends: the Nguyens.

Temporarily. Just for now.

Is there anything anymore but Now? There *was* Then. But that world was blown up in an intersection.

I hear logistics being discussed.

At Jamison, they believe the Nguyens reside at the Gardens of Glenwood, which is where Dell lives.

Everything decided today is TEMPORARY.

Again. So that we all understand.

Temporary. Brief. Not permanent. Provisional. Passing. Short-term. Interim.

We all get it.

The temporary arrangement means I must go to Jamison once a week. And I will continue to see Dell Duke as my counselor.

I have been placed on a leave of absence from school because I told them that I didn't want to go. No one wants to make me do anything right now. They are afraid that I'll run away again.

Dell Duke has agreed to supervise my homeschooling. He looks guilty when they ask him how I'm doing in my class work.

I think that he might say something about the tests and why I had started going to see him, but he doesn't.

I don't care whether he lies or tells the truth.

It's all taking me to the same place.

Dell drives us all back to Happy Polish.

Everyone is exhausted and silent.

Pattie Nguyen signed all kinds of things back there. So who knows what she just agreed to?

The Old Me would have read every word of that paperwork. The New Me couldn't care less.

I'm out of there, that's all that matters.

The sunlight has a way of dulling the world in Bakersfield, and I gaze out the window and everything is like a copy of an original.

The whole place is faded.

It all looks like it would be easy to tear apart.

I'm surprised when we get back to the nail salon and it feels familiar.

The strong odor of the colored lacquers can be smelled out on the sidewalk, even with the door shut.

I'm certain that it is carcinogenic.

Before the world came apart, this would have been a concern.

Now I take a deep breath and hold the noxious fumes in my lungs.

Bring it on. All of it. Bring it on.

Dell hangs around for a while but he's just in the way.

I can see that he's pleased with himself as he finally says good-bye and walks to his car.

At Jamison a lot of people thanked him.

And he looks like someone who hasn't been thanked very often.

One of his shoes is untied but, with his belly leading the way, he has a new swagger in his step.

I don't see anything anymore, but I can't help but notice.

According to Pattie Nguyen, who seems to have seen her share of heartache, activity and a glass of water cure almost anything if you give it enough time.

So she makes me drink two glasses of water.

Then she sits down next to me and says:

"I will help find a good place for you. I will not let them take you until we do. You have my word. You will stay here until we have the answer."

I would like to express my gratitude, but I can't.

Because I can't express anything.

I only nod.

Pattie gets up from the table and starts unloading little square bottles of nail polish into the back cupboard.

People usually find a good place for stray dogs, or for the elderly when they can no longer go up stairs or use a can opener.

Finding a good place for a kid seems like a much bigger challenge.

chapter 29

A memorial service for my parents is held in a
neighborhood community center on the second Saturday after the accident.

Dell drives me there and Mai and Pattie come too.
Quang-ha has other plans, and I watch him head down
the alley with what look like bolt cutters in his backpack.

Lenore meets us at the community center and I see
the nurse from Jamison who helped me when I hit my
head.

I can't look at them.

I can't look at anyone.

As we walk to the front doors, Mai takes my hand. It
feels warm.

It is colder than normal and a sea of mostly unfamiliar
faces press too close, saying some version of how sorry
they are.

I'm not sure that I can breathe. The air is sticking at the
top and the bottom of my lungs.

They put me in the front row.

Workers from my dad's union organized this event and three people are speakers.

I do not hear a single word that they say.

On an easel next to the podium is a poster-size picture of my mom and my dad taken back when my dad had hair and when my mom was skinny.

They have their arms around each other and they are laughing.

I know this picture.

It sits at an angle on my mom's bureau in a frame made from seashells.

I remember when I was younger asking my mom why they were so happy in the photo, and she said because they knew one day I was coming into their lives.

It wasn't logical, but it made sense.

After the service everyone is given white balloons and we are ushered outside.

The helium-filled inflatables say **JIMMY AND ROBERTA** in chunky purple letters.

The idea is to release them while some guy in a suit (but also wearing sandals with white socks) sings about love being the answer to everything.

I watch in horror.

I know for a fact that the latex lumps will end up tangled in electrical wires.

They will find their way into rivers and streams, and even travel for miles out into oceans, where they will choke fish and endanger marine mammals.

But I cannot find my voice to do anything about these future calamities, because it is someone's idea of inspirational to release the bobbing weapons.

Out of the corner of my eye I see a toddler refusing to let go of his helium prize.

His parents finally manage to pry the ribbon from his clenched fist.

As the four-year-old sobs in agony, I know that he is the only one here who understands.

A small article with a postage-stamp-size photo of me is in the local paper, and a fund is started for my future education.

My father's employer makes a generous contribution.

There are other people on the list of donors, but they are only names I've heard in passing, not associated with faces that I would easily recognize.

The only person I know is Jairo Hernandez from Mexicano Taxi Company.

I write Jairo a thank-you note and he calls Happy Polish Nails. It's two and half weeks after the accident. I used the stationery from here, so he took a guess that they might know where I am.

Pattie is surprised that a man wants to speak to me.

I explain he is an old friend. He *is* a friend. And a lot older than me. So I'm not lying.

Jairo asks how I'm doing, and then he says:

"I want you to call me if you need a ride somewhere."

I say:

"Thank you. I will."

It is quiet for a long time but I know he is still on the phone line. Pattie is watching me so I nod and try to look like I'm listening to more than silence. I finally say:

"Did you enroll in school?"

He says:

"I haven't done that yet."

He then asks:

"How is school going for you?"

I could just say fine, but it feels wrong, so I say:

"I'm taking a break from that."

He says:

"Me too."

I add:

"But I'm going to the library today. Maybe that's some kind of start."

I hang up the phone, and later in the afternoon I ask Pattie if I can go to Beale. She says yes.

Once inside the building, I go upstairs and find the spot behind the doughnut chair. I crawl back there, but I don't sleep at first. Instead, I watch the world from this protected place.

The library has regulars.

A lot of them talk to themselves.

But they do it quietly because quiet is enforced here.

After a long nap, I go back down to the first floor.

The computer room is the most popular space in the building.

I'm surprised, but a lot of the people who I think might be homeless (from the amount of things they are forced to leave downstairs at the front desk) go online.

I can see that they check their Facebook pages.

I watch these people click through pictures and view the same kind of videos as the bored-looking teenagers who show up once school is out.

I'm not sure why this is reassuring, but it is.

I go outside and sit on the steps.

I'm not waiting.

I'm just being.

Time exists only in my mind.

For someone grieving, moving forward is the challenge.

Because after extreme loss, you want to go back.

Maybe that's why I don't calculate anything now. I can only count in the negative space.

I'm on a different planet now.

I only speak when I absolutely have to.

Otherwise, I do my best to be invisible and stay out of the way.

No matter how hard they try, other people do not understand because I'm incapable of communication.

And that is why the deepest form of pain comes out as silence.

Mai, when she's not at school, or with her friends, talks to me about her life.

I listen. But I don't answer.

I spend most of my day with Pattie.

She's there for me.

And just being there is ninety-nine percent of what matters when your world falls apart.

I know for a fact that Quang-ha hates me.

But I'm okay with that.

I have brought nothing positive into his life. Now he has to wait longer to use the bathroom, and the hot water in the shower runs out more quickly.

I try to do everything last, but sometimes it doesn't work out that way.

I don't want to cause trouble, so I haven't said anything about being a vegetarian. I just push the chicken or the pork pieces off to the side and then later transfer them to a napkin, and then at the end of the meal I sneak them into the trash.

I know that I'm eating meat bits that escape this tragically simple procedure, but the principle of my decision is intact, even if the reality is compromised.

All reality, I decide, is a blender where hopes and dreams are mixed with fear and despair.

Only in cartoons and fairy tales and greeting cards do endings have glitter.

I somehow make it through the first month.

I dress and brush my teeth when they tell me to.

And I experience the hollow feeling of complete loss, which is emptiness.

Meaning has been drained from my life.

I force myself to think of anything but the one thing that I'm actually always thinking about.

And that is so exhausting that I sleep more than I ever have.

I am a shadow.

I no longer dream in color.

I don't count by 7s.

Because in this new world I don't count.

Chapter 30

⟨✑⟩

I t was dark nowadays when Dell got home to the Gardens of Glenwood.

The only greenery in the apartment complex was in the courtyard.

And that was in a circular patch of red volcanic chips that hurt Dell's feet, even when he wore thick-soled shoes and was just trying to take a shortcut to the always-strange-smelling stairwell.

The pumice rock minefield was dotted with stubborn weeds armed with sharp thistles, which poked up through the cheap layer of thin black plastic under the brick-colored lava bits. The thorns caught Dell's exposed, fleshy ankles and drew dots of blood.

There were no natural glens in all of Bakersfield. It was a flat, dry place made green only by sprinkler systems.

Maybe that was why so many apartment complexes around town were named for ferns and wet, wooded sanctuaries.

It was "an expression of the yearning of a moisture-challenged climate"—at least that's what Willow had told him when she had first asked where he lived and he responded, he had to admit, with puffy pride:

"The Gardens of Glenwood."

Now he took the stairs to his second-floor unit, because the elevator, which was required by law, never worked.

Dell tried, in desperation, to add up the events of the long and challenging month.

A week after the accident (as he had predicted) his supervisor asked to see his file on Willow Chance.

Dell may have found the missing kid on the day she left Mercy Hospital, but he wasn't a hero for very long.

Now, weeks later, he was afraid. He could admit that, at least to himself.

He had given Willow practice exams in everything from the required three-hour test for application to medical school to fourteen of the SAT Subject II's.

And she had aced them all.

But he made the decision not to hand those materials over.

What he sent to his boss was a simple electronic form that revealed next to nothing about the girl.

Somehow, he'd been caught up in so many layers of deception:

Willow Chance wasn't a cheater.

Pattie Nguyen wasn't an old family friend.

The Nguyens didn't live in the Gardens of Glenwood. (Why couldn't they use their own address?)

He didn't homeschool her (like he was supposed to do).

And he had never been committed to being any kind of a counselor.

Willow walked from the nail salon to the district offices on Tuesdays.

She was always on time.

Instead of taking tests or analyzing the stock market, the two now sat in silence.

Dell tried to think of things to motivate her, or at the very least ease her distress, but so far, he had been a failure.

Yesterday Willow had come in and for fifty-five minutes (which seemed like fifty-five hours) Dell worked on a one-thousand-piece jigsaw puzzle of bowls of jelly beans.

Willow didn't place a single piece.

But he knew she wasn't trying.

And he was really bad at puzzles, so it was a struggle in all ways.

After she had gone, Dell opened his computer and wrote up a report.

He knew now that he was being observed. And if there

was one thing Dell Duke understood, it was that he didn't do well under scrutiny.

He had made a mistake by ever getting involved with the genius kid.

Because it was a lot easier to do his job and not care about anything.

And now he cared about everything.

⟨∾⟩

Pattie Nguyen hadn't enrolled in any of the necessary classes for foster parenting, and she didn't go to the one group session that had been offered.

She intended to.

But somehow, more than four weeks had passed and she had yet to do more than check in with Lenore Cole, who was Willow's social worker.

As the darkness of an autumn sky pressed in through the glass of the salon, Pattie looked down at her calendar.

A hearing had been set in family court and a judge would make a determination about Willow in the next two months.

But Pattie decided that today wasn't the time to think about the future.

Today was the day to order more shades of red nail polish.

She found the new catalog from her most reliable supplier and circled a shade that she thought Willow would approve of.

It was called "well red."

Just doing that made Pattie feel marginally better.

Chapter 31

Vietnamese is spoken here.

I can understand the manicurists, even the ones who talk fast.

They never whisper back and forth about their customers' nails.

They talk about their lives.

While they file and buff and paint, I hear their stories, which are nearly all about husbands and children and other family members.

Many of them are related to one another. Cousins and sisters. Mothers- and daughters-in-law.

They are a tribe.

They don't know that what I hear is hurtful. Because even as they complain about bad men or lazy kids, the pain for me is seeing how they are so connected.

To one another.

And to their families.

And to the world.

These women wrap themselves in their stories from the

minute they walk through the glass door until the second they leave at the end of the day.

They use words to build something that is as real as cloth.

And while they complain in lower voices, about one another, they are joined by blood and circumstance and shared experience.

They are part of something bigger than themselves.

Even if they don't realize it.

I do.

I have seen trees that survive fire.

Their bark is burned and their limbs are dead branches.

But hidden under that skeleton is a force that sends a single shoot of green out into the world.

Maybe if I'm lucky, that will one day happen to me.

But right now, I can't see it.

Pattie is at the front desk.

Everything in here is white. The reception area. The manicure chairs. The floor.

White = clean.

I'm pretty sure that with the exception of the color red, Pattie would be pleased if every other shade in the world disappeared.

That's how she sees things.

She has schedules and rules and methods and every day she does her best to impose these on the world, one chipped fingernail repair at a time.

My mother used the old expression "There is a place for everything and everything should be in its place." But she didn't practice it.

Pattie does.

I would say that, with the exception of me sitting in the back of this salon, she's winning the battle.

Pattie is adding up something on a calculator when the phone rings. After she says hello, I hear:

"Today?"

I look over because I'm now an expert in her voice, and while it was even and unemotional, I still heard something different in it.

The person on the other end of the phone line is doing all the talking.

Pattie shoots a look to the back of the salon and our eyes connect.

This must be the call where she officially gets rid of me.

I hear her say:

"I work until six thirty."

Pattie looks out the window. She's struggling now.

I want to make this easy for her. I get up from my spot in the back and I fold up the furniture pad. I close my computer and I take off my glasses.

I breathe deep.

I know that I've been nothing but a problem. I've tried to be invisible, but just my presence here has changed the dynamic of the situation.

Quang-ha was mad before, but now he's a volcano when we cross the alley at night to the garage.

Mai puts on a good front, but even she seems tired of the whole arrangement.

I need this to be easy for Pattie.

She has been good to me.

So I turn to face her and I do my best to smile.

I want this smile to say that I am grateful for what she's done for me.

I want it to say that I'm sorry for being broken.

I want it to say that I understand her situation.

So I'm trying. I really, truly am.

But my teeth stick to my lip and my whole mouth quivers.

Pattie sees my creepy grin and turns away.

I hear her voice, shaky now, say:

"We won't be there until six forty-five. Is that too late?"

Pattie hangs up, and right away dials a number.

Her even disposition is one of her best qualities. And she's maintaining it. Sort of.

Maybe that happens when you've been through a lot. All of your edges are worn off, like sea glass.

Either that, or you shatter.

Bakersfield is 130 miles from the Pacific Ocean, but twice I drove to the beach, just outside of Santa Maria, with my parents.

There was a short period of time when I was obsessed with the study of the ocean, since it takes up more than 70 percent of the planet.

But on the two times that we went to visit, I was afraid.

The unpredictable current and the vast, complex system of wildlife that resides beneath the churning water gave me hives.

Literally.

I was a body of bumps.

So I admire Pattie's composure.

I knew that my time here wouldn't last long.

And today is the proof.

I find myself always waiting for bad news now.

So it's almost a relief to get some.

I walk to the front counter. I hear Pattie saying:

"A woman called from child services. They are doing a home visitation. Today."

Once I'm close, she shoots me a look and then hits a button and suddenly Dell Duke's voice is on speakerphone.

"Well, it's pretty obvious you don't live at my place!"

Pattie only shrugs and says:

"It's temporary."

He says:

"Why did we use my address? What's wrong with where you live?"

Pattie ignores the question. She says:

"Let's start by taking a look at your apartment."

I hear Dell slamming something. His fist into a file cabinet? His head onto his desk?

"I can't just leave. I mean, I'd have to take a sick day or—"

Pattie hits the speakerphone release button and Dell's voice is cut off. She then says:

"Come get us. We'll be here waiting."

She puts the receiver back into the cradle and returns to her work. She says again, to no one in particular:

"Temporary."

chapter 32

‿‿

It isn't long before Dell's Ford swerves into the parking lot. He gets out of his car as if his hair is on fire.

I should be freaking out like Dell, but I find myself mimicking Pattie's attitude.

My edges are gone.

I'm sea glass.

If you look hard, you can see right through me.

There isn't much discussion.

Pattie and I get in Dell's car and we drive across town.

Ten minutes later we arrive at 257 Heptad Lane.

I look up at the apartment house. It appears to be a building constructed by a blind contractor who didn't use an architect.

The proportions of the place are all off, and not in a provocative way.

It looks like someone took an enormous box, painted it the color of serratia marcescens (which is a rod-shaped, pink bacterium that grows in showers) and cut holes in the sides.

I'm somehow not surprised that Dell Duke lives here.

We follow the counselor up a dark stairwell to the second floor, where he opens a door. He's mumbling now:

"I wasn't expecting company. I'm not prepared for visitors. I need to put a few things away . . ."

He then quickly shoots like a trained hamster through a crazy maze of stuff.

We hear a door shut in an unseen hallway.

I wonder what he needs to hide, because there is enough here in his living room that should mortify him.

Dell Duke is obviously one of those people who have issues throwing things away.

Maybe he doesn't have full-blown disposophobia, which is hoarding, but he's on the same playing field.

The Old Me would have taken a lot of pleasure in a firsthand look at such a complex emotional condition.

But not now.

Pattie and I stand in the entry and stare at the stacks of newspapers, magazines, and mail surrounding the discount lawn furniture, which I decide is the exact color of a white rabbit's eyes.

Pink with a drop of yellow mixed in.

The complete patio set—called "masculine salmon" on a manufacturer's tag sticking out from one of the cheap metal chairs—has cut distinct circles in the wall-to-wall carpeting.

I step deeper into the room so that Pattie can close the door, and I find myself next to an outdoor umbrella still encased in cloudy plastic.

It is propped against the wall.

I feel its sadness.

I trail behind Pattie down a narrow path to the kitchen.

Towers of sloppily rinsed microwave trays are on most of the counters. Off to the side, I see teetering columns of red disposable cups.

I realize that I have not had great exposure to other people's ways of living.

I had never seen the kind of garage setup that the Nguyens have going, and looking at this place, I understand that there are clearly whole lifestyles that have been kept from me.

Dell Duke is charting a different course.

If this is what he has in the open, I'm now curious to look in one of his closets.

Pattie must have the same thought, because she moves out of the kitchen, through the clutter of the living room, back to the tight hallway.

I follow.

But with some caution.

This looks like the kind of place where an unexpected

exotic animal might appear—the illegal kind that people buy on a whim in the back rooms of pet stores, but then later set free in an alley because they can't control the razor-sharp claws or the eating demands.

The door to the first bedroom is closed but that doesn't stop Pattie from turning the knob and opening it.

We both now see Dell stuffing an oily-looking sleeping bag into a nylon sack.

But there are no dead bodies or anything.

At least not in plain sight.

It's just a super-messy room.

Comic books and magazines are strewn next to the bed, which doesn't have sheets or a mattress pad.

The necks of empty wine bottles poke out of a metal garbage can (the sort that should be outside) in the corner.

It only takes an instant for Pattie to find the handle on the closet door.

Dell shouts:

"No!"

But it's too late. Pattie has opened the louvered door to reveal a wall of underwear.

There are hundreds of them.

I used to enjoy estimating quantities, but not anymore. I know with certainty that in the past this would have really interested me.

Pattie steps back as Dell sputters:

"I'm . . . behind on the laundry!"

This is truly an understatement. Pattie looks from Dell to the underwear and then to me.

It seems obvious that there is no way that it could ever appear that Pattie and her kids live in this apartment.

But I'm wrong.

I'm not sure what flipped her switch, but maybe it's the size of the challenge.

We are back in Dell's dusty Ford now heading (under Pattie's direction) to the Salvation Army on Ming Street.

Minutes later we all stand at the front counter of the secondhand store.

Pattie has picked out a red Formica table with four nondescript dining chairs, a stuffed lemon-colored sofa, and a leather lounger that swivels in a complete circle.

She has the tags for a metal frame bunk bed with mattresses that appears to at one time have belonged to a military enthusiast. Worn SEMPER FI stickers cover most of the railings.

It isn't until Dell's credit card is out that he has the courage to ask:

"How are we going to get all this stuff back to my place?"

Pattie, without explanation, heads straight out the glass

door to the sidewalk, leaving Dell to complete the trans-
action.

Dell and I find her standing outside at the curb next to
a truck that says WE HAUL.

The two men who get out to help us are named Este-
ban and Luis. They have well-developed packing skills.

It doesn't take them long until they have all the furniture tied down into the back of the very worn-looking
pickup.

Upon arrival at the Gardens of Glenwood, the two men
carry everything up the flight of stairs to Dell's apartment
without even breaking a sweat.

Pattie supervises.

Dell stays out of the way.

I'm the silent observer.

Now all we have to do is get rid of his junk.

Pattie thrusts a detailed list into Dell's hands and orders
him to the market.

Once he is gone, she positions me with Luis and Este-
ban in a line where we form a human chain.

There are only four of us, but using this ancient means
of transport, months of trash leaves the building.

Dell returns two hours later and most of his stuff is

now in the building Dumpsters. He says it was his plan to take it to the recycling center.

But I know that he's lying.

He doesn't seem upset that we got rid of his things, so I guess he's not a hoarder.

He just has trouble with follow-through.

chapter 33

〜

Mai *stayed after* school on Fridays to participate in a program for at-risk teens.

They didn't call them that, though. They called them "special enrichment students."

But of course she knew.

Mai had read the pamphlet describing the funding for the project. It was on the desk of the Team Leader the day of the first meeting, so she wasn't really snooping or anything.

She was curious what they thought she was at risk for.

Once a week a dozen chosen kids met at the school library to discuss everything from setting your sights on college to the importance of getting your teeth cleaned.

Today a woman was talking about eating green vegetables and doing extracurricular activities to build a résumé.

When she finished, they were all given little tickets. At the end of the program they could turn them in for prizes or something. The Team Leader wasn't clear on that.

Mai loaded her backpack with new books from the school library and walked to the bus stop.

Most of the kids who weren't "at risk" had their own cars to drive home, or parents who picked them up.

So maybe, Mai thought, the risk part involved riding the city bus.

The bus shelter in front of the school had a flowerbed with the toughest roses in Bakersfield.

Or at least that's what Mai thought as she stared at the thorny bushes. One of the few things that Willow had said in the last month was that everything in life could be seen in a garden.

According to her, if a plant was in decent soil and had sun and enough water, a bud would at some point show up. It would start small and very green.

Sometimes bugs ate holes in the exterior of the bud, but if they didn't get too deep into the thing, it would bloom.

And the world would see the flower.

With time, the outer petals would start to wrinkle, beginning at the tips. The shape couldn't hold and the whole thing would open up big and then sloppy.

The rose was now more affected by the wind or the rain or even the hot sun.

The petals would finally just dry up, and break away, falling to the ground.

That left only a round bulb, which was the skull of the thing. And in time that would finally drop as well, returning to the soil.

There was as much of a lesson in that, Willow had explained, as in anything she had been told by anyone about life or death or the stages in between.

What was the rose before it was a rose?

It was the soil and the sky and the rain and the sun.

And where was the rose once it was gone?

It returned, Mai figured, back to the larger whole that surrounds us all.

⟨✦⟩

No one ever picked up Quang-ha from school, so when Dell Duke's car screeched to a stop right at his feet, he was alarmed.

The smudged window slid down and Dell shouted:

"*Hey!*"

The boy could feel his whole body tense. You don't say "Hey" to someone named "Ha."

And then Dell shouted:

"Get in! We're on a tight schedule!"

Quang-ha didn't budge.

"What's going on?"

Dell reached across and opened the car door.

"Ask your mother. She's running this scam."

Dell didn't explain much; just that Pattie and Willow were at his apartment fixing it up to make it look like they lived there.

It all seemed pretty shady to Quang-ha.

But he called his mother on her cell and she told him to load up the cooking stuff from their garage.

He was supposed to take blankets and sheets and bathroom things too.

He was pretty sure it was the dumbest idea in the world, but he crossed the alley and took the sweaty counselor with him.

For over a month Quang-ha had been sleeping in the same room with a complete stranger. Maybe someone was finally going to do something about that.

Dell stood in the doorway of the garage and stared.

No wonder they had used his address! This place didn't even look legal.

Dell had assumed they lived in a house or at least a real apartment. So this was a shocker.

Where did the woman get all of her attitude?

After he and the Lone Wolf (who might actually be an Oddball) had placed a rice cooker, a bamboo steamer, a wok, half a dozen bowls, tongs, a collection of chopsticks, two meat cleavers, three cooking pots, and the bedding into Dell's trunk, they filled an old milk crate with food.

They then grabbed some stuff from the bathroom in the salon, and were back on the road.

It felt, to Quang-ha, like some kind of prison break.

By the time they swung into the dusty carport of the Gardens of Glenwood, he was even more on board with the whole plan. It seemed obvious that they were going around the law, or at least defying some rule or regulation.

And that was exciting.

chapter 34

Is there a more personal piece of clothing than someone's underwear?

I don't think so.

Dell wears all different styles.

He has a great variety of colors and a shocking number
of patterns. He is heavy on the cartoon characters. And
images of vegetables.

It is truly disturbing that I now know this.

This man is not just my counselor. He's also supposedly
monitoring my schoolwork. Although in five weeks, that
has never once come up.

I can't believe we don't just leave his privates in the
closet, but Pattie is all about doing things the Right Way.

Even if that means getting involved in someone's
obsessive-compulsive underwear disorder.

It takes us three trips to haul the mountain down to the
laundry room.

After we get the first load started, Pattie morphs into
some kind of human tornado.

Earlier, I realize, she was just some kind of tropical storm.

By the time Dell and Quang-ha come up the stairs carrying the box of kitchen stuff, we have mopped the floor (which turns out to be shades of orange, not brown), cleaned the microwave and all of the counters, and filled eight trash bags with more detritus.

I know a lot about bacteria and germs, so this is all very challenging for me.

Dell has barely finished bringing up the stuff from the garage when Pattie hands him another list and shoves him back out the door.

Quang-ha stays with us.

Everything in Dell's apartment looks gray.

This is because someone put a canvas tarp over the skylight in the living room. Probably to cut down on air-conditioning costs or something.

Now that tarp is coated in atmospheric dirt. Mold and mildew stains rim the edges where water must collect.

So when you are in Dell's living room, no matter what the weather is outside, overhead it appears that a CAT-5 hurricane has just descended.

Pattie has her hands on her hips and she's squinting up at the covered skylight.

She says:

"It's not right."

The look on Pattie's face isn't good.

I stare up with her.

It's like a giant dirty diaper is on the ceiling.

She calls for Quang-ha, who has just been given a large plastic garbage bag of wine and beer bottles (found under the bathroom sink) to take downstairs.

Pattie points skyward.

"I want you to go up onto the roof and take off the tarp."

In a month, I've never seen Quang-ha happy, so his current scowl is just more of the same. He says:

"You just told me to throw away these bottles."

Pattie says:

"Do both."

I feel bad for him and offer:

"I'll help."

Quang-ha doesn't want my assistance. But his standard operating procedure is to ignore me. Completely.

And I'm okay with that.

Now he grabs the heavy bag and heads to the door.

I follow.

We are both in the hallway and he's lugging the bag of bottles. He should leave them if he's going to go up on the roof, but he doesn't.

I don't say anything because he's older and can't stand me. And also because I rarely talk now.

He's only here cleaning up Dell's because of me and my problems.

There's a stairwell at the end of the corridor, and a sign indicates that it leads to the roof.

I wish that Quang-ha would put down the bag of bottles. I think he's trying to prove something to me, like maybe that the big bag isn't too heavy for him. But I know that it is.

I've lifted more things today than I have in the last six months.

Quang-ha goes right up the narrow steps. There is a door at the top with a sign that says:

ROOF ACCESS FOR MAINTENANCE
WORKERS ONLY

I don't think we qualify, but Quang-ha just pushes the door open anyway. The sun is sinking, but outside it is still bright. There are ten skylights and ten dirty old tarps.

So Dell isn't the only one with interior shades of gray.

I can see that Quang-ha is confused.

I point to the left side of the building.

"Over there. The third one is his living room."

He isn't going to argue with me because after over a

month of living together he knows I really only talk to state facts.

Quang-ha still has the garbage bag as he moves across the hot roof.

Again, I follow him.

I'm not sure why. I'm his little kid shadow and I can see that I'm only making everything worse.

There are bricks that hold down the corners of the tarps, and when we reach what is Dell's unit, I lift one.

Quang-ha then bends over and, with his free hand, pulls on the dirty piece of canvas.

But the trash bag slips from his other hand and the bottles spill out and one crashes right at his feet.

Green glass shards go flying and several pieces land on the clear plastic of the newly uncovered skylight.

The Old Me would have screamed from the crash.

The New Me expects these kinds of things.

The New Me is actually surprised that we weren't cut up from the airborne shards.

Quang-ha was angry before. Now he's *really* angry. He starts to pick up the broken glass.

I move quickly to help.

Standing over the skylight, I see that three glass pieces have caught the sun. They send small spots of color down into the room below.

I glance over at Quang-ha. He sees it too. I say:
"It's like a stained-glass window."

Quang-ha is silent, but he takes a beer bottle and breaks it. He then positions a piece of amber glass on the surface.

A chunk of orange-brown light now hits the carpet below in Dell's place.

We exchange looks.

But we don't say anything.

And then we go to work covering the entire skylight.

We end up breaking all of the bottles to get enough glass pieces.

I find this to be strangely enjoyable.

I can tell Quang-ha feels the same way, even though he is silent while we smash what appears to be the result of a real drinking problem.

When we finally finish, we go downstairs.

Quang-ha opens the apartment door and we both can see right away that the room has taken on a totally different quality.

The light.

Chunks of green and amber filter down from above.

What was an ordinary and soulless feature is suddenly interesting.

We're standing there staring up at what we've done

when Pattie comes in. I don't want her to be mad, especially at Quang-ha. I say:

"It's temporary."

I'm surprised when Pattie only says:

"Quang-ha, you can arrange the furniture if you have a better idea how it should go."

I'm *not* surprised when he does.

Quang-ha puts everything in a different place, setting the couch and the chairs on an angle. He doesn't follow the lines of the rectangle room; he makes his own shapes.

And when he's done I want to say:

"There is a qualitative difference in the visual effect of the room."

But instead I say:

"The room looks better."

Quang-ha just shrugs, but I can see he's not scowling anymore.

This is the first thing we've ever done together, and I realize that it feels strange.

For both of us.

And I'm forced to admit that being in a room with a teenage boy who appreciates the effect of shattered glass slices of color makes me feel better about the world.

chapter 35

D ell pulled his name out of the mail slot for
#28, replacing it with a slip of paper on which
Quang-ha had artfully written *Nguyen*.

He then made a beeline for his car, driving away just
moments before Lenore Cole pulled up to the curb.

He headed straight for the closest bar, which was called
the Hammer. Most people in Bakersfield went to the
Hammer when they crashed their car or lost electricity in
a heat wave and had all of their ice cream melt.

The bar was a misery magnet. No one put on their best
sweater or their skinny jeans to go to the Hammer.

That's why Dell felt at home there.

Now, as he drove into the parking lot, he let out a sigh
of relief. He had gotten away from Pattie Nguyen.

Dell found himself mumbling out loud as he opened
the car door.

"Who died and put her in charge?!"

Then he remembered that two people actually had
passed away. And maybe he was the one who had inad-

vertently put Pattie Nguyen in charge by getting her pushy daughter involved.

All Dell really knew with certainty was that now someone was steaming mounds of spinach in a kitchen that had never under his watch seen a vegetable in its raw form.

At least his underwear wall was being washed.

Once inside the dimly lit bar, Dell found a seat. As he leaned forward onto the sticky countertop he took a pen from his pocket and slid the thin cocktail napkin closer.

He was looking to regain control, and so he returned to the Dell Duke System of the Strange.

He wrote:

1 = MISFIT

2 = ODDBALL

3 = LONE WOLF

4 = WEIRDO

5 = GENIUS

And then he added his newest category:

6 = DICTATOR

Mai had to take a second city bus across town to the Gardens of Glenwood.

And she was not happy about it.

She called her mother from the salon and that was when she found out about the visit from child services.

Shouldn't someone have told her what was going on?

Now, an hour later, Mai's arms ached from carrying her heavy backpack.

But inside she felt a different pain.

She had to question the logic of pretending to live in Dell Duke's apartment.

Maybe Willow should have gone right after the accident into foster care.

Her mother had made it clear. They weren't in any position to take on another kid.

She had tried to help, but what if what she had done ended up hurting Willow even more?

Mai aimed her right shoe, which wasn't more than a satin slipper, and stepped down hard on an acorn.

But the nut lying in the middle of the cracked sidewalk didn't squish under her foot.

Instead it was solid and tough and it hurt. It was like stepping on a pointy rock.

Mai felt her whole body stiffen.

So many things caused unexpected pain.

Mai kicked the acorn and it flew across the sidewalk out onto the street. She watched as a passing car ran right over the still-green nut.

Mai moved to the curb to get a better look.

The acorn hadn't flattened. It rested on its side in the middle of the road, unharmed.

Mai dropped her backpack and went to retrieve it.

The acorn was a survivor.

Mai stuffed it into her pocket.

Lucky. That's what the nut was.

When Willow wasn't paying attention, Mai would slip it someplace she would find it.

chapter 36

❦

I'm exhausted.

I've helped transform the apartment of a single, lazy, hoarding hermit into a family's living space.

And this has been done insanely fast.

Now as the bamboo steamer gets going, and Pattie has me chopping up green onions, the buzzer rings.

Lenore Cole is downstairs.

Once a week, since the accident, I've gone out to Jamison.

I've had a complete physical exam. I've had three sit-downs with a psychiatrist (Dr. Ron McDevitt) and I've seen Lenore Cole twice.

There's been talk of permanent placement in foster care, but it's not easy finding spots for older kids.

I met a girl in the bathroom during my visit last Thursday who said that once your baby teeth fall out, no one wants you.

She also told me that prospective parents always pick the blond kids first.

I don't think that she was trying to be a bully or any-thing.

We both had hair the color of ink.

The social worker isn't with us long.

Which is a good thing.

I guess we passed the test.

Pattie's not trying to be a foster parent, but still, they have requirements, even for the temporary custody people.

In the hallway, Lenore Cole says:

"We will find the right place for you. That's our mis-sion."

I don't answer.

I want to see this lady out the front gate and into her car and off the street and out of town and then removed from the county and then the whole state and finally relo-cated to the place they call Tornado Alley in Kansas.

But it's not her fault.

I'm the Problem.

Maybe there are all kinds of available foster homes in Kansas.

I'm in the shadows of the entryway watching as the social worker gets in her car and pulls away from the curb.

She drives right by Mai.

Just seeing the graceful teenager changes everything for me.

When I tell her that we have a pretend room complete with Semper Fi bunk beds, she rotates in her shell.

She doesn't have an actual shell, of course, but whatever hard casing that protects her from life literally shifts before my eyes.

Apparently, she's long wanted to climb a metal ladder before she goes to sleep.

Maybe it's from years of sleeping on a floor.

I don't want to disappoint her by saying that all of this was just for show so they wouldn't haul me away.

Once in the apartment, I thank Pattie for everything she did today.

To my great relief, she is finally sitting down.

The world's ultimate pragmatist just shrugs and says:

"Những gì mình mong ít khi nào nó xẩy ra. Những gì mình không muốn thì nó lại cứ đến."

This translates to mean:

What we expect rarely occurs; what we don't expect is what happens.

I reach over and take Pattie's hand. I'm surprised as I

do this. I'm too old to be acting this way, but I can't stop myself. I manage to say:

"It's not a scientific way to view event sequence, but given what's gone on in my life, I completely understand."

It's the most that I've been able to communicate in a long time.

And I'm not sure if I'm just tired, or if something has changed, but as I look at her, with my hand in hers, I smile.

My teeth don't even stick to my lips.

And Pattie doesn't turn away.

Everyone is really hungry, even me, and I never have an appetite anymore.

Pattie tries to reach Dell, but he doesn't answer his cell phone.

So we have dinner without him.

Then what's especially strange is that suddenly it feels as if we all really do live at the Gardens of Glenwood.

We eat our food at the red linoleum-topped table and toss the paper plates (Dell doesn't have real ones) in the trash.

Pattie has Quang-ha immediately take down the garbage to the Dumpster because the kitchen is a trash-free zone now.

We all help clean up and put away the leftovers, and then we make ourselves at home on the newly acquired, used furniture.

I can't believe that she has the energy, but Pattie starts to fold Dell's mountain of clean underwear into tight, compressed squares.

They look like they come out of some kind of vending machine.

That's how precise she is.

Quang-ha is in love with Dell's large TV and he finds a program where Japanese soccer players use their heads to smash clay pots.

We all watch.

It is strangely addicting.

I know that these blows to the skull can cause long-term health issues of a very serious nature.

But right now that seems like the last thing I should be worried about. So I let it go.

For a brief moment, because everything in this room is so different, I forget that I don't have a mother or a father or a place to call home.

I lean back on the sofa.

And I feel a sharp pain in my right hip.

When I put my hand there I realize that I'm sitting on a small, green acorn. I have no idea how it got on the couch.

Apples grow on apple trees. And cherries grow on cherry trees. But we don't say that an acorn grows on an acorn tree.

Things like that are interesting.

At least to some people.

I hold the little nut (which is by definition a fruit) in the palm of my hand. Mai is next to me, and she smiles as she says:

"Maybe that's a lucky acorn."

I slip it into my pocket, because maybe she's right.

It is a seed, after all, and they are by definition the beginning of something.

I then rest my head on the back of the sofa and even though my eyes are all watery, I can make out the full moon as a fuzzy amber-and-green lollipop on the other side of the skylight.

And that's not a bad thing.

chapter 37

I t was late when Dell finally stumbled into his apartment.

He literally didn't recognize the place, and not just because Pattie was asleep on the new Salvation Army couch and Quang-ha was sprawled out on the carpet nearby under a red blanket.

Dell shut the door and moved into the hallway. Willow and Mai could be seen sleeping in the second bedroom in the Semper Fi bunk beds.

He wondered why they hadn't all gone home, and then he remembered they didn't have a car, and right now, neither did he. He'd walked home.

After staring in wonder at all the changes, he finally made it to his room, where his bed was made up with Pattie's sheets and a fluffy comforter.

Dell planted himself, face-first, on top of the mattress.

And that's where he was only five hours later when the sound of the shower in the bathroom woke him up.

It was not a normal noise.

He'd never heard running water in his own apartment.

Dell opened his eyes and realized the sound was from the bathroom. He squinted at the digital eyes of his bedside clock and saw 5:21 A.M.

Who would get up this early?

It was one of *them*. And he had a good idea which one.

Dell would have given his left foot for another hour of uninterrupted sleep.

He shut his eyes and suddenly saw himself minus everything below the ankle on his weaker side.

That made him wonder if the injury meant he'd collect some kind of disability payment from the school district.

He used his right foot to drive, and most people did, so he guessed the left foot didn't bring in as much cash in a settlement.

Isn't that the way insurance companies worked? Everything had some kind of predetermined price?

Maybe it was better to give up a left arm.

And then there was a knock on the door and the *Dell Duke Internal Idiotic Discussion Forum* was interrupted by the voice of Pattie Nguyen.

"Are you awake?"

He wanted to say that he was *now*. Instead he answered: "Been up for hours."

He hoped it sounded deeply sarcastic, but she answered: "Me too."

Pattie pushed the door open and entered talking:

"Social Services is coming back next week. Until they find a permanent place for Willow, I think that it would be easier if we just stayed here. I can't keep cleaning up after you."

Dell was silent. Not because he didn't have an opinion but because he didn't have the energy this early in the morning to scream at the top of his lungs.

Pattie forged on:

"I saw a notice on the board in the laundry room. Unit 22. Just down the hall. Looking for a roommate."

Dell shut his eyes. This had to be a dream.

Except that in his dreams, usually he was hiding. And often his body had mysteriously been painted bright blue.

Dell opened his eyes. Pattie was already heading to the door.

"I'm going to get the e-mail address. It's not too early for you to send a message saying you are interested. It's temporary. Just until we get this all straightened out."

Dell had seen Sadhu in the parking garage, but they had never even so much as said hello.

Now at an insane hour of the morning he was sitting across from the man. The crazy Nguyen woman had insisted that he send an e-mail right away and then to his horror his laptop showed an immediate reply.

The guy who was just down the hall wanted him to come over right away and meet.

Shouldn't the man be asleep?

What was wrong with all these people?

Sadhu cleared his throat and said:

"I'm a vegetarian."

Dell nodded. Sadhu looked suddenly hopeful.

"You are a vegetarian too?"

Dell shook his head. He wasn't going to lie, but he also wasn't going to go into detail about his meat loaf obsession.

Because Dell was so tired, he looked appealingly like someone who had been to mime school.

Or at the very least, believed strongly in the power of nonverbal communication.

His answers were a series of head movements, punctuated by yawning, raised eyebrows, and semi-swallowed hiccups.

And that is why he was approved as a roommate.

Minutes after he took his seat, Pattie Nguyen came down the hall and wrote Sadhu Kumar a check for one month's rent for the second bedroom in unit 22 in the apartment complex where Dell already rented unit 28.

She would cover his expenses living with Sadhu, and Dell would continue to make the payment on his place.

As he shook hands on the deal, Dell found enough of a voice to make a statement. He said:

"Spicy food gives me indigestion."

Sadhu nodded his head as if he understood, but Dell felt certain the guy was pickling peppers on his stovetop.

Chapter 38

⌒

It's all just "temporary."

That's what Pattie says.

I believe this is her favorite word.

What is more temporary than nail polish? No wonder she has such an attachment to the concept.

Pattie explains that until the right place can be found for me, we will all stay at the Gardens in unit 28.

There will be weekly home visitations from Social Services, and the coming and going would be too much.

I don't explain that everything in the world is temporary, because I don't get into those conversations.

I say that I understand.

But I feel bad for Dell Duke.

Not just because Pattie and I saw his underwear mountain (which maybe is why he agreed to move down the hall).

Back home, when I used to sit in my garden, I liked to observe birds, and not just the green-rumped parrots but also the migrating species.

I think now about how small birds often move in large flocks.

From a distance, it can even look like smoke.

It is unclear why they suddenly shift directions.

The birds appear to have lost their individual intention.

They are part of a bigger organization of life.

And they accept that.

Something inside them gives in. Scientists don't know what that is.

Right now I'm in a flock.

And so is Dell Duke.

Whether he likes it or not.

I watch as Dell gathers together some of his clothing, his toothbrush, and a container of what looks like hairspray.

He heads down the hallway to Sadhu Kumar's apartment with a heavy step.

He's not stomping, but it's close.

Who can blame him?

Two hours later, with Mai and Quang-ha awake and helping, Dell's work clothes, as well as his oversized sweatpants, his collection of sandals, and enough underwear to last six months, are all jammed in the Kumar apartment's second bedroom in the tiny closet.

Only a garbage bag of old T-shirts stays behind.

And since Dell's bureau and closet are empty, Pattie borrows his car and brings over more things from the nail salon.

Mai goes with her.

I don't think that I've ever seen my teenage friend so happy.

Dell has a huge TV, but he hasn't programmed it correctly.

I adjust the settings and now everything isn't all stretched and too bright. I also fix it so that the audio is in sync with the picture. It wasn't properly aligned before.

I notice that over 70 channels haven't been activated.

I don't think he read the manual.

Dell comes in and sees the changes and says that people do look better not so orange and wide. He especially is pleased that when they speak, their lips match.

I show him the new channels that I've programmed, and he gets angry because he's been paying for a year for premium services.

He's pretty worked up about it.

I know for certain that we will now have things to talk about in our weekly counseling sessions, because he's asked me to review every appliance in the place.

Tonight the new living arrangements take effect.

Mai and I still sleep in the second bedroom. Pattie is

now in Dell's old room. Dell is down the hall at Sadhu Kumar's.

Quang-ha has officially taken over the living room. He has blankets and a pillow on the couch because he sleeps right in front of the big TV.

And I mean right in front.

This could cause eyestrain.

But he looks so thrilled with everything about this new arrangement that I don't bring it up.

I wake up in the Semper Fi bunk bed this morning to the realization that I'm going to need to pull my own weight.

At least as much as a twelve-year-old kid can.

My parents didn't have life insurance, or much in terms of a savings account.

They were responsible and hardworking, but it turns out they didn't excel in the long-term planning department.

I will start by putting Pattie's accounting from Happy Polish on a new computer program.

Everyone has made sacrifices for me.

I feel that it's the least I can do.

Three days have passed.

Maybe it's some kind of joke, but Quang-ha leaves an avocado pit in the window ledge in the kitchen.

Apparently he loves guacamole.

Mai says when Quang-ha was little he put toothpicks in the sides and tried to grow avocado trees. Quang-ha then gets mad and throws the pit in the garbage can.

I have not thought about cultivation since Before.

It's too painful.

But when no one is looking, I rescue the avocado pit from the trash. I almost cry just looking at the thing.

Suddenly, I can't help myself. I start to think about soil composition.

I try to push it out of my mind.

But later, when I glance out the window, my eyes fall on the scrubby trees across the street.

Three different species.

I consider the possibilities of grafting the woody stems from one plant to another.

I'm lying in bed.

Everyone is asleep.

It is late.

Night is always the hardest.

The shadows pull you under.

I hear a dog somewhere outside barking.

I shut my eyes, and instead of darkness, I see rooting hormones.

I have placed what Mai calls "my lucky acorn" on the box next to our bunk beds, which serves as a nightstand.

I open my eyes and stare at it.

The world of plants is a slippery slope.

It's hard to care just a little.

chapter 39

It's the weekend.

I come into the living room. Quang-ha is sprawled out on the sofa, moving from channel to channel as if being paid by the number of programs that he can simultaneously track.

His agitation is some kind of internal struggle.

But it isn't muscular, it's mental. I know the difference.

He doesn't take his eyes off the television, but he says:

"Are you looking for something?"

I want to say that yes, I'm looking for anything that could make a world gone flat return to its original shape, but instead I just mumble:

"No. I'm getting a glass of water. Dehydration is the cause of ninety percent of daytime fatigue."

Someone is knocking at the door.

It's Saturday and Pattie's at work. Mai is out with friends. Quang-ha and I are both home at the Gardens.

I go open the door and Dell's standing there. He starts to say something, but nothing comes out.

I know how that feels.

This is all weird for so many reasons.

We live in Dell Duke's apartment. And he has to knock to even come inside.

Pattie set down some ground rules on Thursday. She is tough. She actually took away his key because he locked himself in the bathroom the second day for over an hour and he should be using Sadhu's from now on.

But I pull open the door for him, which is welcoming. If we were in the wild, I would part the leaves of the tree and move back on the branch.

He takes a step inside.

Quang-ha shouts over his shoulder:

"Whatever it is, I didn't do it."

Quang-ha has a real persecution complex, which is no doubt legitimate.

The chubby counselor says:

"I don't have a television down the hall. I'm missing all of my shows."

Quang-ha answers:

"You can watch with me as long as you don't do anything nasty."

I see Dell's face soften. I think he likes the word *nasty*.

I'm invisible now, which is fine with me. Dell moves closer to the big-screen TV, asking:

"Do you watch a lot of sports?"

Quang-ha's response doesn't seem like a joke:

"Not if I can help it."

This is the right answer, because Dell seems relieved as he drops down onto the couch.

It's a real thud and I feel bad for whoever lives underneath us.

I didn't have siblings and my dad never had friends over to hang out on the couch and talk back to the television set.

But that's what's happening now.

So this is all new to me.

Dell takes out a pair of fingernail clippers from his pants pocket, and while Quang-ha flips through the channels, Dell pulls off his socks and clips his toenails.

I don't think you would do that if you hadn't lived here before.

I retreat to the shadows of the kitchen.

Instead of staring off into space or sleeping, I watch.

Since the accident, I feel next to nothing about everything, so it is possible that this surveillance will be beneficial to me from a psychological standpoint.

But probably not.

The teenage boy and the man are as close to wild animal observation as anything I've seen.

I realize that this is a unique opportunity to get insight into both of these people. Not that either of them is very mysterious.

But I'm looking for understanding of bigger things.

Like the human race, as an example.

Right away I notice that Dell and Quang-ha scratch more than girls.

They are slumped down in their seats and appear to be really concentrating on the televised programming.

On three occasions I hear what can only be described as "aggressive laughter."

After the third outburst, they each make a fist and bump knuckles.

For a nanosecond I'm fearful this signals a fight.

But it's just the opposite.

The knuckle touch is a bond.

I know for a fact that these two people don't even like each other.

Is the television programming bringing them together?

Why would watching a group of out-of-control young women in bathing suits competing in a canoe contest do this?

I conduct my surveillance from the shadows next to the purring refrigerator. It is silent, motionless observation.

They seem to have forgotten that I'm in the apartment. Their behavior appears completely reflexive and natural.

Quang-ha has the television remote, and he moves through the channels in a way that a grandmother might turn the pages of a speedboat catalog featuring water skis.

There is not much stopping for analysis.

Dell and Quang-ha appear to be hunting for two things:

Mostly they are looking for acts of violence. (They watch with great amusement as a man in a cartoon gets stabbed in the eye socket with an ice pick.)

The rest of the time they seem to be stalking the airwaves for appealing females.

When they find either thing, they stop to enjoy the visual stimuli.

They call girls "hot."

The girls are not untouchable, like truly high-temperature objects.

No.

They mean attractive.

Dell even yells out "Super-hot."

And I hear Quang-ha say "Smoking!"

It all seems very inappropriate.

There is a whole language to be learned here.

This is an education.

After a while I've had enough and I go downstairs to be outside.

I need fresh air.

Growing up, unless it was raining hard, I was outdoors for part of every day.

Now I want to sit in my old backyard, which was in some ways a jungle.

But of course I can't do that.

Even though this place is called the Gardens of Glenwood, there are nothing but weeds and the dusty pumice rock in the central open area.

I take a seat on the steps and stare at the layers of stone, which look (from a distance) like heaps of red potatoes.

I shut my eyes and as long as I keep them closed, I'm surrounded by greenery. I can feel the plants swaying in the wind and the ground alive below me.

I used to be somewhat of an expert on earthworms because a good garden holds so many kinds of life.

Over the years, I made homemade paper from tree pulp, and I've mashed grapes with my feet (but it was easier to use a blender).

We harvested a lot of what I grew.

Now I listen to the dryer tumbling in the laundry room. And someone's radio. I can't help but hear bits of an advertisement for a place that sells discount tires.

The guy on the radio doesn't know I lost my parents. He's just selling cheap rubber wheels.

The person who put the clothes in the dryer has no idea that I need a foster home.

Overhead I hear the sound of a jet engine, and I open my eyes and look up in time to see the plane pass by high in the sky.

I'm thinking now about the passengers on board.

I'm wondering about them and their lives.

Are they looking down out the windows next to their seats?

Do they see a two-story apartment building that is an unappealing color of pink?

Do they give a thought to the people inside?

Do they feel a girl sitting on the steps trying to make sense of the world?

I seriously doubt it.

Who wants a seat at my pity party?

I get up and head out the gate to the front of the apartment complex.

I see a hummingbird in a bottlebrush tree that is

planted in the space between the sidewalk and the street.

I make a decision and head upstairs.

Dell and Quang-ha barely look up when I enter. They are watching girls play beach volleyball. Very intently.

I go to the kitchen and I boil four cups of water. This releases the chlorine. I then add one cup of sugar, which easily dissolves because of the heat.

I wait for the mixture to cool.

This is what I used in the past to feed hummingbirds in my garden.

Now I pour the still-warm syrup into a bowl and I go back downstairs. But first I put on my red sun hat.

Outside, I take a seat right next to the flowering bottle-brush tree.

I dip my hands into the sugary mixture and I sit very, very, very still.

It takes a long time, but a ruby-throated hummingbird finally descends and eats from the tip of my unmoving, sweetened index finger.

I've heard that there are places that hold statue contests.

But I'm certain that they aren't anywhere near Bakersfield.

I will see only what I want to see.

It's possible that's how people get through crisis.

The world where we live is so much in our head.

If I'm sent by the state of California to foster care in a remote location with no Internet and no books and no vegetables, where I will live with a family who secretly worship Satan and only eat canned meat, then so be it.

Until then, my life is at the Gardens of Glenwood.

And I'm thinking this place needs a real garden.

chapter 40

◦~◦

It happens, as most things do, in the smallest of ways.

I take a few clippings.

I'm not thinking about what I'll do with them.

I'm getting out of Dell's car three days later and the monthly maintenance man has trimmed the lone jade plant by the front entrance of the apartment building.

A few of the cut pieces are still on the ground.

I pick them up.

I take the clippings inside, and place them in a water glass.

The light is good by the front windows. It's south-facing.

I have my counseling this morning.

I walk from the nail salon to Dell's office and I realize that I'm looking at the lawns and the trees and the flower-beds as I make my way there.

I haven't seen them until today.

I know it's not possible that all of this stuff was planted in the last week.

What have I been looking at for the last six weeks?

I arrive at Dell's office and we pretend, as always, that nothing has changed and we don't live in the same apartment complex on the same floor of the same neighborhood of Bakersfield.

He doesn't drive Pattie and me to the nail salon every morning.

He doesn't eat dinner with us.

He doesn't watch hours of inappropriate TV with Quang-ha.

I slide into the chair and he says:

"We need to talk about going back to school."

I say:

"I'm not ready."

Dell Duke looks at me, and whatever my face is doing seems to be working, because he shrugs and says:

"Okay."

We spend the rest of the session pretty much staring at nothing. And then right when it's time for me to go, he says:

"Tell me one thing that I can do to make your life better."

I'm surprised when a voice comes out of my body.

"You could get me a packet of sunflower seeds."

Dell leans forward.

"For eating?"

I answer:

"For planting."

He nods. But then he repeats:

"For planting?"

I say:

"Yes."

Pattie and I ride the bus at the end of the day back to the apartment and Dell is waiting for us in the living room.

He's with Quang-ha and the TV is on.

He gets up and takes us into the kitchen.

He has two dozen packets of sunflower seeds spread out on the counter.

I could grow a field of sunflowers.

He says:

"I never knew that there were so many kinds. I wasn't sure what you wanted, so I got them all."

I look down at the sunflower packets and see Honey Bears and Strawberry Blondes. There are Vanilla Ice and Chianti Hybrids. I see Fantasia and Tangina and Del Sol.

He's even picked up a packet of pollen-free bloomers.

I stare at the seed envelopes and it's too much.

My eyelashes collect tears.

For so long I couldn't cry.

But I guess once you learn, it's like everything else; it gets easier with practice.

I know that Dell's not a very competent person.

He's not even a particularly interesting person, unless he's judged by his organizational disorders.

But until this moment I hadn't realized that he's a really caring person.

I don't know what to say.

So I scoop up the seed packets and go straight to my room.

I hear Dell ask Pattie:

"Did I do something wrong?"

I don't hear her answer.

After dinner I go down the hall and tell Dell that I'm going to open a few of the packets.

He comes back to #28 and together with Mai we spread some seeds onto a wet paper towel that I've placed on a cookie sheet.

I then explain that for a few days I will keep these seeds moist.

This will ease the process of germination.

Mai and Dell watch. They look pretty interested.

I tell them:

"Sunflowers are indigenous to the Americas. They came from Mexico."

From the other room a voice says:

"My dad came from Mexico."

Quang-ha pretends he's never paying attention to us.

But apparently he is.

chapter 41

M ai could not remember ever feeling this way.
Maybe it was because her brother hadn't been scowling so often in her direction.

And her mother hadn't been telling her to put her things away.

Mai sat on her bed and appreciated that she had an actual room with walls and a door that belonged to her and to Willow.

At least for right now.

Maybe it was the acorn.

Willow had put it on her night table. The kid was slowly beginning to collect things. She had gathered the small, bead-like pods that fell from the trees on Penfold Street.

She found a white feather at the bus stop and a speckled rock in the gutter out front.

Mai felt like it was some kind of beginning.

She knew that any minute they would be told to pack up their things and leave, but up until the very second that happened, Mai was going to enjoy this new life.

So she took long, hot showers, even though that was wasting water and bad for the planet.

She arranged and rearranged her clothing at every possible opportunity, admiring the hangers and the shelving in the shallow closet.

She stretched her arms out wide when she slept so that they dangled over the edge of the bunk bed.

Because now she wouldn't be hitting a face or slapping the back of a neck.

Mai cut pictures out of magazines and put photos of people she didn't even know, but just liked, up on the walls.

She found a box of red paper lanterns in the attic storage at the nail salon. She bought a string of Christmas tree lights and threaded them through the round fixtures, which she then hung in the bedroom.

It made the low ceiling come alive.

And what she knew for certain was that the weight of the world no longer felt like it rested entirely on her shoulders.

❧

Jairo drove his taxi across town to the college bookstore.

He stood in the long line at the cash register waiting to pay.

Books were expensive. Especially textbooks.

He held the two pieces of required reading for the introductory course in biology against his chest.

They were both used. That was a good thing. Someone had taken a yellow pen and marked up one of the books.

Jairo hoped that the right parts were highlighted.

Just the idea that there were *important* sections of the books and *other* sections that didn't deserve the swipe of the yellow pen made his stomach hurt.

Suddenly, he couldn't do it.

He hadn't been in school in fourteen years.

Now, surrounded by so many young people, he felt old.

Ancient, really.

He was thirty-five years old, but hadn't he recently found gray hair?

Three strands. They grew on the very top of his head, in the center, shooting up from the thicket of black like the rebels that they clearly were.

Those three hairs were outlaws with the confidence that one day they would conquer their world, which was his head.

Jairo was almost at the cash register when he spun around. He should put the books back. Who was he to think that he could take college courses? Why would anyone ever want him to work in a hospital? How would he pay for a degree?

This was all just a big waste of time.

Jairo moved back to the maze of aisles. But the large store was crowded and he suddenly couldn't remember where the books had come from.

And there was no way that he was going to just dump the textbooks on the wrong shelf. He wasn't going to be *that* guy.

Settle.

New plan.

Just buy the things. Owning them didn't mean he'd go to class. Maybe he could read the stuff in his spare time. Didn't he have to wait every day of his life for people?

Who was he kidding? That wasn't happening.

Could he give the books away as gifts? They were used and had yellow pen marks all over them. What kind of present was that?

Jairo leaned back on his heels and allowed his eyes to close for just the briefest of moments.

He needed to talk to her.

His angel.

She'd appreciate the textbooks.

It was with her on his mind that he stepped back into the line for the third cash register.

The young woman behind the counter rang up his purchases, and when he handed over the cash she hesitated. Did she look surprised? People didn't seem to pay that way. The woman hit a button to make the register drawer open.

Suddenly a light swirled and a buzzer went off.

Everyone stared.

At him. At the clerk. At the spinning red ball up front.

What had he done?

Jairo felt his face grow hot and then he saw someone who looked official pointing in his direction. The cashier was giggling as she said:

"You're our one millionth customer."

He had no idea what she was talking about. His expression was blank. She filled in with:

"You won! Didn't you hear about it?"

Jairo shook his head.

Other workers were now assembling and a man in a burgundy jacket appeared at his elbow. He had a pin on his chest that said MANAGER. He held up a camera.

"Smile!"

Jairo tried his best to make his quivering mouth form some kind of grin.

And then he heard a voice from somewhere in the small crowd say:

"He won twenty thousand dollars, man! And I was right behind him in line. Unreal."

Jairo looked around and realized that the cardboard triangles suspended from the ceiling all said:

ANNIVERSARY CELEBRATION!

BE OUR 1,000,000TH CUSTOMER AND WIN!

A woman held her phone close to his face as she said:

"Can you tell us your name? Are you a student? What are you studying at Bakersfield College?"

He realized now that she was recording him. He managed:

"I'm a new student. This is my first time here."

The crowd gave a collective groan, followed by laughter and chatter.

"His first time! Come on. I've spent a fortune in this place!"

As the woman continued to question him, Jairo became conscious of the fact that he was smiling as he spoke.

And he couldn't stop.

After he filled out all kinds of forms—from the bookstore and from the government for taxes—they officially took his picture.

This time holding a big oversized check.

And then he was given the real thing.

Everyone was so nice to him. He was slapped on the back and he shook hands with dozens of students. He hugged people he'd never seen in his life.

Finally, as he walked back to his taxi, moving across the wide parking lot in the midday sun, he checked his watch.

He'd been inside the place for almost three hours.

But in his back pocket, folded in half in his worn-shiny leather wallet, was a slip of paper worth a year's salary driving his taxi.

And that money would pay for all the college classes he ever wanted to take.

chapter 42

Every weekend Pattie goes to a farmer's market on Golden State Avenue at F Street. She likes to be one of the first ones there.

Today Mai went with her because Pattie's using Dell's car and they can get more things and she'll help carry the stuff.

They are going to pick up two bags of potting soil for me at the nursery on the way back.

The best way to grow sunflowers is in the ground, not in pots or planters. They have enormous taproots that burrow deep.

My plan is to start them off in small containers and then locate a place later for transplanting.

Dell and I go through the big blue recycling Dumpster in the carport and we find twenty-three containers for me to use as planters.

We pick out an assortment of tin cans, a few plastic tubs (that once held sour cream and spreadable cheese), and even a few milk cartons.

I don't think I've seen Dell so happy as when he's rooting around in the Dumpster.

After we have what we need, we go to the laundry room and wash the cans and containers in the deep sink.

Then Dell punches holes in the bottoms with a kitchen knife, which gets ruined because you're not supposed to use it for that.

He doesn't seem to care.

When Pattie gets back with the potting soil, we are going to plant nine different types of sunflowers.

But another thing happens when we are readying our potting containers.

Sadhu Kumar, who rents his extra bedroom to Dell, comes down with three computers. Dell says:

"What are you doing with those?"

Sadhu is getting ready to toss them into the big blue bin.

"They're going into the recycle."

I size up the machines. They don't appear very old. I ask:

"You can't fix them?"

Sadhu snorts. Like a horse might do.

"They are junk. Not worth the effort."

I look at the computers. Two are laptops. One is a larger desktop. But the same company makes them all.

Sadhu Kumar is sort of an angry guy. I think he might have had a lot of disappointment in his life. It can turn a person bitter.

I wonder if that's happening to me.

Nothing's worse than a sour kid. You should save that for later. When you are old, and it hurts just to get up from a chair, you have a reason to have a permanently pinched face.

I make a note to myself to be sad, and even mad, but not one hundred percent angry at the world.

There is a difference.

Now I ask Sadhu:

"So I can have the computers?"

Mr. Sour Bitter Man says:

"If you want junk, take junk."

Dell Duke looks offended. He says:

"One man's garbage is another man's treasure."

Sadhu only seems more pained at that thought as he walks away.

We are still waiting for the potting soil, so Dell and I carry the three machines up to #28 and right away I start to take them apart.

I think that I might be able to get one working computer from the three.

I see that it could be possible to use the logic board from the first one, and the chipsets and plug-ins from the other two.

I'm not sure it will function properly, but if it does, the computer will be a gift to Dell from me.

He doesn't know that yet.

I'm at the kitchen table separating the peripheral wiring when Dell Duke's cell phone barks.

He's chosen a dog as his ringtone.

It doesn't seem like what a cat person would do.

It bothered me while we were cleaning up this place that I didn't find a single thing to indicate that Cheddar had ever lived here.

This is a man who couldn't be bothered to throw trash away.

I've been waiting for the appropriate time to bring this up. Once he's off the phone I ask:

"Do you miss Cheddar?"

Dell looks confused.

"Say again?"

I repeat:

"Do you miss Cheddar?"

Dell's eyes narrow.

"You mean, because Pattie cooks Vietnamese food?"

I don't respond. He adds:

"What I miss is my meat loaf."

I'm not going to follow up.

Pattie and Mai return and we're ready to begin.

Pattie says she'd like to help us, but she's testing some

kind of new nail polish and it wouldn't be fair to the product to stick her hands in dirt.

I'm surprised when Quang-ha comes downstairs to do the planting.

He picks out a container. (It is cloudy plastic and previously held strawberry-flavored imported Italian gelato.)

I must admit that judging by the shape, this is the most intriguing of our Dumpster planters. It is rectangular, but has soft edges.

Quang-ha is confusing because just when I'm certain he has sawdust for brains, he'll exhibit some real insight. He picked the best-looking container for his seedling.

While he obsessively pulls off the stickers from the sides of the former gelato carton, Mai and Dell and I fill up everything else with the fresh dirt.

When he's finally ready, I hand Quang-ha the cookie pan, which has the moist seeds, and I say:

"Plant three. Equidistant. About an inch down."

Maybe he doesn't hear me, because he takes a single seed. I say:

"Take three."

He mutters:

"I only want one."

I don't want to be bossing anyone around. Especially him. I say:

"It might fail. They are only going to be in these containers for a short time. We are just starting out here."

He will not be persuaded. I can't read his expression, so maybe he's making fun of me as he says:

"I'm putting all my hopes and dreams into this one seed. That's how I want it."

Dell is now watching. His mouth opens and I think he's going to say something. But he doesn't. Mai then turns to her brother.

"We're doing this for Willow. Don't be a jerk. She wants us to plant three seeds."

Quang-ha looks from Mai back to me.

"This one is mine. I'm not doing it for her."

Dell turns to us.

"You two girls do your own thing."

I get a lump in my throat.

And it's not because Quang-ha won't listen, or because Dell doesn't support my planting methods.

I feel moved because they aren't treating me like I'll break into a million pieces.

Maybe that means I'm on my way back to some kind of new normal.

chapter 43

❦

I can focus again.

If only slightly.

It doesn't take long for a routine to really fall into place.

We all get in Dell's car every morning.

We drop off Mai and Quang-ha at the high school and then Dell takes Pattie and me to the salon.

Most days Mai walks over after school and then she and I ride the bus to the Gardens of Glenwood.

Pattie stays later, but is home for dinner.

Mai and I get things started for the evening meal. Pattie can't just walk across an alley to cook anymore, and a lot of her dishes take time.

This means that we're in the kitchen in the afternoon, which opens right up onto the living room.

I can't help but observe Quang-ha, and later Dell when he gets home from work and positions himself next to Quang-ha in front of the TV.

The two somehow understand each other.

Maybe because they are both on the outside of something.

I'm invisible to them, unless it comes to Quang-ha's homework.

I helped him with a math problem, which is how it started.

I can do his assignments in a few minutes, but I take a lot more time than I need so that he won't feel bad.

I know that doing his schoolwork is morally wrong, so I try to explain basic concepts before I hand over the material.

I can't say that he is a good listener.

His only serious activity, besides watching anything on the TV, is doodling.

He draws cartoon-like people with large heads.

Quang-ha has a somewhat large head.

I'm not sure if there is a connection.

Every day Dell asks me when I plan to go back to middle school.

I want to say:

"How does *never* sound?"

But I don't.

Instead I usually pretend not to hear or mumble something that has a few indistinct syllables.

Today Dell adds:

"There's a lot you are missing there."

I can't help myself. I say:

"Name one thing."

Dell looks confused.

But it's not a trick question. I really want to know.

I can tell that while Quang-ha is changing channels, he's paying attention. He can't stand high school. Finally Dell says:

"You don't go to P.E."

I just stare at him.

Dell's belly looks like he has a basketball under his shirt. Yes, he's lost some weight in the last month, but he's got a long way to go before he's any kind of athletic specimen.

But it's as if he's some kind of mind reader, because he says:

"I'm going to start running. Tomorrow is my first day."

Quang-ha shoots him a look of total disbelief, but I'm the one who says:

"Really?"

Dell nods. I say:

"Are you training for something?"

Dell says:

"I'm going to be joining some teams in the spring and I want to be in shape."

Quang-ha is giggling now. Not laughing. Giggling. It's different. It is suppressed and high-pitched and contains an element of disbelief.

I've never heard Quang-ha giggle.

It must be a very unusual sound, because the next thing I know, Mai is out of the bedroom and standing in the hallway.

"What's going on?"

Quang-ha starts to answer, but he can't. He is a giggling mess.

Somehow, this form of high-pitched laughter is contagious, because Mai is now giggling. She's watching her brother, and whatever he's doing is spreading.

Dell has had enough.

He gets up from the couch and goes into the kitchen.

I follow him.

We stand there. We can still hear the giggling in the other room. I say:

"Are you really planning on running?"

Dell mumbles a form of yes. But then adds:

"But I'm not going to join any kind of team in the spring. I made that part up. I'm just going to run for myself."

I don't think that's strange because almost everything that I pursue is for my own understanding or amusement.

I believe having an audience naturally corrupts the performance.

I might be self-justifying.

But I say:

"I think that is a great idea."

Dell says:

"Let's go water the sunflowers."

The next afternoon, Dell does run.

He makes a big show of it, coming in dressed in what looks like a costume, not an athletic outfit.

Quang-ha starts the giggling thing again.

I manage to say:

"Good luck out there."

And then Dell's gone.

He comes back in bad shape.

He's soaked in sweat and he's as red as can be.

And he was only gone eleven minutes.

I don't keep track of time anymore and I don't count, but I saw the clock on the stove when he walked out the door.

I just happened to be looking in that direction when he came back.

I say:

"How was it?"

Dell is breathing very, very hard. He holds up a hand. It's the international signal for *stop*.

I give him time to regain a somewhat regular breathing pattern. Finally he says:

"Very tough. I might be a little out of shape."

From the couch I hear the return of the giggling.

I write a five-page paper on Mark Twain over the weekend for Quang-ha.

He is very resistant to certain aspects of learning.

I believe that he understands a lot of what is being
taught, but he has no interest in doing the work that
comes with the assignments.

Maybe he's just too tired from his late-night TV viewing.

I don't think Pattie realizes that once she's asleep, he
turns the thing back on.

He somehow got himself a headset, so the sound just
goes right to that.

I know because I spend a lot of the nighttime awake.

Quang-ha is clever enough to delete the first paragraph
of the Mark Twain paper and go through the computer
file and misspell a dozen words before he prints it out.

But it wasn't enough because he comes home today in
a very bad mood.

He's being moved out of his English class and put into
some kind of Honors/AP program.

I will not take the blame for this.

Chapter 44

P attie had to find something for Willow to do. It was the only way to keep her from staring off into space.

She didn't like the look on her face when that happened.

The girl was so still. Like a statue.

Or a dead person.

In the nail salon she could scare the customers.

So Pattie gave Willow the lease agreement for the salon, and the kid actually read it. She pointed out three areas with inconsistencies, and made a document for Pattie to use when she next met with the landlord.

It was impossible not to be impressed.

When Pattie casually said that she wished she had room to add another manicurist, Willow made a floor plan of the nail salon that optimized the space, moving the front counter and three of the four manicure stations. This opened up room for a new chair and foot spa.

Pattie immediately took action.

And the crazy thing was that it felt less crowded, not more, once they added the new person.

But the kid was obsessed with disease and infection.

She saw problems that didn't exist, and it grated on Pattie's nerves.

She finally told Willow to just write down all of her anxieties.

The next day, when Willow handed her a detailed report on the incidence of infection from manicure and pedicure treatment, Pattie got angry. She had never had a single complaint from a customer with a health problem.

Pattie avoided the twelve-year-old for the rest of the day, sending her back to the apartment early.

But then that night Pattie had a dream.

It was a gruesome nightmare in which her clients all keeled forward, face-first, onto the manicure desks.

The next morning, Pattie asked Willow to talk her through the information.

Her eyes glazed over when Willow spoke about new drug-resistant bacteria, but she got the gist of the whole thing.

That afternoon, new, more powerful disinfectant was purchased for the basins and foot spas.

Willow insisted that it never be watered down, as they

had done in the past to make the chemicals go further.

Pattie had all of the manicurists stay an hour late that night, and Willow gave them a presentation (in Vietnamese, which was impressive for that reason alone).

The following Monday, once the changes were all in place, Pattie let Willow post the ten most important health rules that every nail salon should follow.

Pattie put Willow's manifesto on the front window, and she adopted the girl's proposed new slogan:

SETTING THE STANDARD IN CALIFORNIA

FOR HEALTH AND SAFETY IN NAIL CARE

But Pattie was still surprised when new customers began appearing.

Willow had said that it would happen.

❧

Dell no longer ate meat loaf.

He wished his mother were still alive, because he wanted to tell her. He was certain that she went to her grave worried about his addiction to compilation meat dishes.

Hadn't he discovered a list in her address book written just weeks before she died?

It read:

1. Find a pair of high heels that don't hurt my feet.

2. Cancel life insurance.

3. Get Dell to stop eating so much crummy meat.

It had taken a decade since he first saw her spidery handwritten list, but now it was a fact.

The meat obsession was behind him.

He didn't cook his meals anymore, so he wasn't sure that he could take any credit for the change.

But still.

There had been other life improvements.

He had a new computer.

Technically it was an old computer, or at least a machine made from salvaged parts, but it was faster and more efficient than any other piece of equipment he'd ever owned.

Willow had made it for him.

When he brought the new-old computer down to #22 and Sadhu saw how it worked, the guy's eyes almost popped out of his head.

It made Dell proud.

Now he adjusted the pillows behind his back and opened his computer to his secret file.

It was late and he couldn't sleep.

But not like before from severe indigestion.

He didn't have a TV in his room at Sadhu Kumar's, so he had to read or work.

He clicked on the screen, and the Dell Duke System of the Strange appeared.

He needed to add a new category.

Dell's fingers slid across the keys and he typed in:

MUTANT.
Color code: blue.
His favorite color.

Next to MUTANT he typed the word: ME.
Dell shut the computer and stared up at the ceiling.
He was changing. He was capable of that.
He decided that all his life he had been influenced by things around him.
Now he lived with a cranky man who was originally from Punjab. And when he wasn't with him, he was down the hall with the Californian Vietnamese.
He was identifying.
Since he was usually self-destructing, this felt so peculiar.
But he knew that he was now different.
And it wasn't just the little things.
Sure, he now trimmed his beard. He'd raised the bar on his personal hygiene in a lot of areas.
But that wasn't the mutation.
It was bigger than that.
It was on the inside.
Because the truth was that, as frustrated and angry as

he first felt, he had to admit that once his junk was all gone, and the rest of his things were put into some kind of order, he had started to feel stronger.

Pattie had taken over his apartment and moved him down the hall, but that, too, had an upside.

Because for the first time, in as long as he could remember, Dell belonged to something.

Even if he was the one that they all talked about behind his back, it still made him part of a group.

They were playing on the same team.

Pattie had fixed the buttons on his shirts and had offered him a free pedicure at the salon (with one of the girls who was in training).

When he didn't show up she scolded him, prompting Dell to clip his toenails down so close it hurt to even put on his socks.

But then she gave him foot lotion and powder to sprinkle in his shoes, and that made his toes smell fresh like lavender or something sweet.

Before, his feet smelled pretty rotten.

And then there was the running.

That started out as a lie. He hadn't planned on jogging anywhere.

But now it had been two weeks.

Every day after work he came back to the apartment

building. He put on the orange tracksuit that he'd had since high school. It didn't fit anymore, but he could still squeeze into the pants if he kept the waistband low.

Then he set his watch for twenty-two minutes and he headed out the door.

In his comic books, the Mutants had secret powers.

It was possible, he now thought, that he did too.

Hadn't he and Pattie managed to take care of Willow Chance?

That was pretty powerful for someone who couldn't even keep a houseplant alive.

Chapter 45

The sunflowers are coming up.

We planted seeds in twenty-three containers, which have pretty much taken over the kitchen. And we have germination in all of them.

I don't make a chart and monitor the percentage of germination, because I don't do that anymore.

But it crosses my mind, which is interesting.

Dell and Mai are both excited when they see the small, green seedlings.

Before I can stop him, Dell gets all gooey and over-waters everything.

Quang-ha acts like he couldn't care less, even though his single seed sprouted and already looks bigger than the others.

I find a doodle of the seedling on a pad of paper near the TV.

It's very precise, so Quang-ha had to have gotten very close and taken a real look at his new plant.

In his picture, the seedling is growing out of the top of a man's large head.

I'm not sure why this pleases me so much. I say:

"Quang-ha, do you think I could have this drawing?"

His eyes don't leave the television. He makes a noise, which I can only describe as some form of a grunt.

"Is that a yes?"

He waves his hand in my direction.

I take it to be some sort of positive gesture because there are no fingers involved.

I put the drawing of the man with the germinating brain in my room on the wall where I can see it when I roll over.

Mai is very happy that I have something up, even if it's just a picture that her brother drew.

She has been decorating since the first day we moved in.

The Helianthus annuus are fine for now in their containers, but they will need to be transplanted.

Quang-ha hears me refer to the sunflowers in this way and laughs.

Teenage boys are so easily amused.

But very soon the H. annuus will all need more space.

I don't want to talk about relocation. It's too uncomfortable all around.

My social worker has told me that they are actively looking for a foster parent to take me.

I've had three home visitation checks.

All three were fine because we do all now live at the Gardens of Glenwood.

For now at least.

I'm here on a temporary basis, but each day gives me more time to adjust to my new reality.

So I need to be grateful.

That's what I'm working on.

Dell comes over for dinner and we eat bún riêu and bánh cuõn. I think Dell is developing a real taste for the food, because he takes seconds on the rice balls.

I pick my way through the meal and when the timing seems right, I say:

"I want to thank you all for what you've done for me."

No one answers.

It's like I pulled a rotten fish out of the refrigerator and placed it on the table. My words have a smell.

Everyone goes from looking uncomfortable to embarrassed, and then Quang-ha just gets up and takes his plate and leaves the table.

I know he wasn't one of my early supporters.

But they don't realize what a difference they've made for me.

Or maybe they do and they are just keeping the knowledge to themselves.

I go to sleep early but I wake up every hour.

In the morning I decide that I've done a disservice to myself in terms of my physical achievement.

This is another way of saying that since no one thinks being motionless for hours is any kind of sport, I'm very challenged, athletically speaking.

I think exposure to something new can't help but generate interest, even if you feel out of it and on your own planet.

Dell comes in this afternoon from his exercise regime and he's red-faced and sweaty.

He may be exhausted, but he looks alive.

I'm interested in that.

So I take a big step. I say:

"I'm thinking of running."

Quang-ha hears me and his weird giggle returns. I don't look at him. I keep my eyes on Dell, who says:

"Really?"

I continue:

"What I meant is that I would like to start training. And I was hoping that you could help me."

Quang-ha is really giggling now, and he's not trying to hide it anymore.

But Mai comes out of our room. She shoots a hard look at Quang-ha and says:

"I'll do it too."

And with that, our running education begins.

I need athletic shoes.

I only wear work boots everywhere, and you can't jog in those. Mai already has running shoes because she uses them in her high school gym class.

The following day, she and I walk to the Salvation Army.

She points to three shelves with used shoes and then disappears to look at a raincoat.

It really doesn't rain much around here, but Mai has strong feelings about fashion and she's spotted some kind of designer rainwear.

I begin going through the shelves, and I'm surprised to find a pair of track shoes that actually fit well.

The Old Me would have obsessed about the possibility of a contagious medical condition being passed on from someone else's footwear.

The New Me has been a patient in a hospital and gotten a lot out of that experience.

So my only objection is that the running shoes are bright pink, with hot-purple laces.

Once I put them on, I feel like a flamingo.

With the exception of the color red, I always wear earth tones because I'm blending into my environment. This is important for observation.

But I'm not in any position to complain, so I smile with my lips closed and say that the flamingo footgear is terrific.

I don't normally use words like *terrific*, so maybe Mai will understand that I have my concerns.

But she doesn't pick up on it.

Our first day of running is tomorrow.

When I get home I work with Quang-ha on his biology.

I give him a single-page document with a distillation of what he should know for his upcoming test. I try to come up with little tricks to help him remember things.

I think it's possible that I have natural teaching ability.

I'm not boasting.

I'm just presenting the facts.

He's starting to exhibit a degree of understanding.

He tried to hide a recent pop-quiz from me, but I found it in his notebook.

He got 91/100. The teacher wrote a note at the top: *Your new effort is paying off!*

I'm certain the last thing Quang-ha wants is to be some kind of biologist, but it's good to see he's not getting sent to the office for threatening to burn people with lab equipment.

All of this leads me toward my own expansion.

I go online and devise a running plan. I show Mai and she appears to be interested.

She says we will go as soon as Dell gets here because he wants to come with us.

I have charted out a one-mile loop that travels eight blocks south of the Gardens of Glenwood.

It then turns three blocks west.

Followed by eight blocks north.

And finally three blocks east.

On the map, it does not look like much.

I'm lucky to still be alive.

After two blocks on the course, I get a pain in my left side that feels as if a knife has been implanted just below rib 7 (individual ribs do not have names, and are only referred to as one through twelve, left side, right side).

My legs—or more specifically, my calves—tingle, and somehow I have lost all of my strength.

My ankles freeze up.

The air around me turns thick.

I experience so many different health conditions—rapid heart rate, elevated blood pressure, dry mouth, pulmonary shock, muscle spasm—that it is impossible for me to even chronicle the degree of body breakdown.

The shocking truth is that I cannot even continuously jog eight blocks south (which was the first segment of the run).

At the sixth block I stumble.

I feel that I might lose consciousness (and there is no metal elephant coffee table to break my fall).

Mai places her hand on my arm and says:

"Take it easy. Just breathe, Willow."

I know it sounds crazy, but as I work to control my wheezing breathing pattern, something happens.

I go from light-headed to feeling grateful for the gift of life.

It must be some kind of blood pressure phenomenon.

Dell and Mai walk with me back to the Gardens of Glenwood.

I want one of them to tell me that I'll get better at this. But they don't.

As we enter the apartment complex I say:

"I'm going to try again tomorrow."

I see Mai and Dell exchange looks of concern.

In that instant I decide that I will exercise (time permitting) each afternoon for the rest of my life.

Maybe I'm more competitive than I thought.

I'm very sore from jogging every day this week.

Except for day four, when I suffered some kind of setback and had to walk the whole mile, almost on my hands and knees, I know that I've made progress.

But I believe it is fair to say that I will never be very good at running.

Here is an even larger truth: I am not in any way a natural when it comes to body movement.

It is in this moment of clarity that I understand that I have never danced.

I know that I was forced to do some kind of folk steps to music in fourth grade, and I now realize that I was tragically uncoordinated even at that.

It's funny how I'd blocked the experience out of my mind.

In order to successfully transition from twelve years old to being a teenager and then to an adult, will I need to be able to move my hips to a song?

I'm sweating just thinking about that.

That's why this running matters.

I think that the *effort* put forward in matters of physical exertion is more important than the outcome.

And I'm not just saying that because gym teachers have told me this in the past.

A new reality is emerging.

I actually like my pink-and-purple flamingo shoes.

So maybe the jarring movement of jogging is clouding my judgment.

Even though my exercise regime only takes sixteen minutes, I find that I'm thinking about it when I'm not doing it.

I know that vigorous exercise changes brain chemistry.

In my current situation, there is nothing more I could ask for.

chapter 46

I'm on my way to the laundry room when I look under the lava rock in the courtyard.

I push away a small section of the heap of surprisingly dirty red stones and then peel back a corner of the torn plastic liner.

As suspected (because of the appearance of the weeds), there is dirt under there.

For the briefest of moments I imagine clearing away the rock and digging a pond to grow water lilies and red bog flowers.

I would plant timber bamboo along the north side to jut up into the open space and shade the roof. I suddenly see vines and lush plants clumped together, and the air is pungent with the smell of life.

But then in an instant that vision is gone.

I'm left staring at the red rock and the thistles.

A piece of black plastic that is close to the dryer vent appears to be waving at me like a black flag.

I go upstairs to report my findings.

Dell is on the couch with Quang-ha. Mai is reading a book on her bunk bed. Pattie is at the salon. I say:

"I have an idea. I want to plant the sunflowers downstairs."

Mai is listening, because she shouts from our room:

"Downstairs where?"

I forge ahead:

"We could remove the red lava rock heap. There's dirt under there. I checked. Think of it——a courtyard with sunflowers."

Dell looks instantly concerned.

"No way. We're not removing anything. This place is bank-owned."

Mai comes into the room.

"The red rocks are pretty gross."

Quang-ha hits a button on the remote and increases the volume.

Dell has to talk louder now:

"No one touches the red rocks."

I say:

"Maybe just one section."

Quang-ha, despite his lack of interest, says:

"My sunflower is bigger than the others. It should go into the ground."

Dell waves his arms.

"Nothing's going anywhere. They can stay where they are and be dwarfs. Or whatever happens to things that don't have enough space."

Mai doesn't like the way that sounds.

"In my 'at risk' afternoon program we had a whole session on seeking permission for community projects."

Dell gives her a crazy look.

"This isn't a community project."

Mai shoots back:

"Of course it is."

Dell changes his argument with:

"I'm too busy right now to get anyone's permission for anything."

He's just sitting on the couch with Quang-ha and neither of them appears to be doing much. Ever.

I then say:

"I'll take the initiative. I can get approval from the bank."

It comes out like a threat, but I didn't mean it that way.

Dell looks more than confused. He says:

"How are you going to do that?"

I send Jairo at Mexicano Taxi an e-mail and he answers right away.

He will pick me up from the salon and take me to

Bakersfield City Hall tomorrow at ten in the morning.

His message says he has news. He's been waiting to hear from me.

In the morning, once we are at work, I wait by the front door of the salon for Jairo. I'm usually in the back, so just being up here makes the day feel different.

Pattie says:

"I'm happy that you have a project."

I nod.

She's always trying to get me to go back to school, without making it seem like she just wants me out of here.

There's a fine line between encouraging someone and telling them to get lost.

I understand that.

I don't say that the idea of leaving the salon for someplace new makes me light-headed.

I'm not good with change right now. I can't even yet make a variation in my mile running course.

Mai suggested that we jog the opposite way yesterday.

That feels like the most radical idea in the world.

I can't risk heading in what feels like the wrong direction.

Jairo gets out of the taxi and comes inside so that Pattie can meet him.

She doesn't like me going off in a car with a strange man. I explain that at this point the taxi driver and I aren't strangers, but I understand her concern.

I can see that Jairo's wearing a Bakersfield College T-shirt.

I'm very happy about this.

I didn't know that Pattie spoke Spanish, but right away they start talking in that language.

I speak Spanish, so I understand as she says what translates to:

"This little girl has been through a lot."

Jairo tells her:

"This little girl changed my life."

Pattie nods, but he doesn't say more. She then gives Jairo her cell phone number and says to call if there are any problems.

This strikes me as strange because I'm thinking that I should be the one calling to report the problems, not him.

But I'm looking out the window and trying to let them have their moment.

Or whatever it is that they are doing.

I realize that Jairo is the first person I've seen talk to Pattie who she hasn't tried to order around.

Interesting.

In the car, driving to City Hall, Jairo asks:

"Did you see my picture in the news?"

I have not paid attention in the last few months to news of any kind.

"No, I'm sorry. Is everything okay?"

Jairo is very excited now. Almost jumpy. I hope that he's watching the traffic and the rules of the road. He says:

"I won twenty thousand dollars. I'm using it to go to college."

I gasp. This *is* news.

He talks nonstop for the rest of the way about my being his angel, and I have to say that by the time I step out of the taxi at City Hall, I'm feeling pretty good about his life.

Jairo says that he will wait outside, and I explain that this could be a long process.

I promise to call him and he finally gives in.

I don't want to tell him that I'm not his angel.

I'm not anyone's angel.

But I do say that I think he will make a fine medical technician. It's an expanding field.

Jairo wants to call Pattie and let her know that I arrived safely.

I don't think that it's necessary, but I say:

"Yes, I'm sure she expects you to call."

I didn't realize that this statement would make him smile, but it does.

The City Hall looks interesting from the outside.

As a rule, I find public architecture stimulating.

I go inside to the information desk and wait until the woman there is off the phone. She finally hangs up, and I begin my quest:

"I'd like to review the documents on file for building projects that come before the city council."

My request seemed simple. But the woman behind the counter obviously doesn't think so. She says:

"Excuse me?"

I repeat:

"I'd like to review the documents on file for building projects that come before the city council."

The woman still looks confused. She says:

"How old are you?"

I answer:

"Twelve."

I can see that I'm about to be the victim of age discrimination. This woman seems to love repetition.

"Twelve?"

I repeat:

"Twelve."

She says:

"Why aren't you in school?"

I have an answer, even if it isn't one hundred percent truthful:

"I'm homeschooled right now."

I want to add that I'm obviously getting an education in bureaucracy every time she moves her mouth, but instead I say:

"I'm interested in seeing what a presentation looks like, and it's my understanding that these things would be part of the public record."

The woman remains suspicious. And not very accommodating. She opens her mouth and this time says:

"Where are your parents?"

Everything stops. I stare. My eyes get drippy and I hear a voice inside.

I repeat it aloud, saying it to the world, which includes her:

"A world lost,

a world unsuspected

beckons to new places

and no whiteness (lost) is so white as the

memory of whiteness."

And then I add:

"William Carlos Williams. 'The Descent.'"

I don't explain how much I like this poem, which is, I think, about aging, not death. But right away I'm directed to the Office of Building and Safety.

I end up talking to a lot of different people.

Finally I'm introduced to a man with a large right ear and an almost nonexistent left ear.

Just a nub, really.

The man has a scar on his neck on the nub side.

He doesn't look like a fighter, so my guess is he was in an accident.

Human ears have successfully been grown on the back of rats and then attached to the head of a human by grafting.

Obviously, I don't bring this up.

But I want to.

The man with the ear issue goes into a back area and returns with a book filled with the notes from hearings.

For a second I find the connection interesting. He's in charge of the *hearings*—and something happened to the outer covering of what he uses to hear.

But I don't obsess on that.

The man watches me with real intensity as I leaf through the documents.

The garden in the center of our apartment complex

does not need the approval of elected officials to be transformed, but I want whatever I submit to the bank to appear very professional.

I spend a good chunk of time for the next two days writing a proposal for an interior garden at our building.

I include drawings (done by Quang-ha under my direction in exchange for biology flash cards).

I include research on the climate of our area, the ideal plants that can be grown here, and a study of the benefits of green areas in living spaces.

I also pull the building permit for the Gardens of Glenwood to show that the interior space has the proper drainage, and that in the original plans, they didn't show rocks, but plants.

It's my first project since Before.

After two days, I have a full three-ring notebook to submit to the bank board.

I believe that I may have provided too much information.

That can be as big a mistake as too little knowledge.

But I can't stop myself from amassing more and more material.

I'm making the request in Dell's name, because he is the person on the lease, and also because getting this kind of detailed plan from a kid would no doubt raise the flag of alarm.

I present Dell with the black binder.

"Here it is. I think you should go into North South Bank. Ask to see the manager. Introduce yourself, and then leave this with him."

Dell is silent as he opens the notebook and begins to look. It doesn't take long for him to say:

"I can't do this."

He shuts the binder and tries to hand it back to me.

Dell Duke is not a bad person. He is just bad at *being* a person.

And he has issues with authority.

Or at the very least, he seems very easily intimidated by anyone who has some. I say:

"We're not asking for money. We're not asking for anything but permission to remove an eyesore and transform a communal place. It would be an improvement."

I've barely gotten the words out of my mouth when Mai comes through the front door. She's been at her friend Kalina's house.

"What's going on?"

I look from Dell back to her.

"I've made a proposal and Dell needs to take it into North South Bank."

Mai has crazy power over people. It only takes one word from her.

"Dell . . ."

He changes course like the wind in a dust storm.

"I'll drop it off tomorrow on my lunch break. Does that work for you two?"

We nod.

From the couch Quang-ha says:

"I did the drawings."

The garden project is under way.

At least on paper.

chapter 47

෧෨

T he new court date was set.

Pattie held the document in her hands.

The system was responsible for children until the day they turned eighteen years old. So Willow Chance had six years to navigate these waters.

Pattie remembered the note that Willow had written the first day she met her social worker at the nail salon. She couldn't imagine that any other kid had presented something as precise.

Willow had a high-functioning brain. That much was clear.

So what does the world do with a twelve-year-old girl without family and a network of close friends? What were the choices?

In the big envelope the social worker had sent, Pattie now found a pamphlet for the next state-sponsored Adoption Fair.

From what she could see, the process looked like speed dating.

The fairs were held in a park. Prospective parents

arrived and mingled with the busloads of kids, who came with social workers.

Hot dogs and hamburgers were served. A softball game was usually organized. The idea was to just be natural and give people a chance to get to know each other.

According to the statistics on the last page of the informational brochure, there were matches made. And of course, sometimes they worked out.

Pattie felt certain that the little kids, especially the cute ones, got all the attention, since they were featured in the pamphlet.

The older kids, even the more outgoing ones who were trying to sell themselves, no doubt ended up the snakes at the petting zoo. People probably kept their distance.

It was hard to imagine Willow Chance in such a setting, but maybe she would defy the odds.

Hadn't she been doing that her whole life?

Mai liked to shop. So even her mother's regular trip to the farmer's market presented an opportunity to browse.

Pattie always bought chicken feet from the man who sold organic eggs. He saved them for her in a special cooler of ice. She used the yellow fowl feet to make a soup that Mai had to admit was delicious, but it tasted better if you didn't see the ingredients.

While her mother went down her shopping list, Mai wandered the aisles of the parking-lot-turned-market, looking at the organic honey and the purple turnips.

Willow said that she used to grow everything that they sold there in her own backyard.

Mai looked at the lettuce and the potatoes and the onions and the red cabbage.

It didn't seem possible.

But Willow wasn't a liar.

About anything.

At the far end of the last aisle was a man playing a banjo. Mai moved closer to hear him.

The sun was shining, but it wasn't the punishing heat of summer or late spring. The air was still cool.

Mai took a seat on the edge of the curb and listened.

She couldn't help herself from imagining the notes of the plucking strings playing for dancing chickens.

And then in her dreamy vision, the birds suddenly were without feet.

Mai stood up.

She felt a growing sense of panic as she looked in all directions for her mother.

It wasn't just the idea of the feet-less fowl that was causing her distress; she now saw sunflowers for sale in tubs in almost all of the stalls.

She hadn't noticed them before.

Each blossom held its own unique possibility.

Willow told her that if they didn't get their small sun-flower plants at home into the ground soon they'd be stunted.

She said that they needed to put down a real root system to achieve their potential.

Don't we all, thought Mai as she hurried toward her mother in the distance.

Don't we all?

❦

chapter 48

Big news.

My binder worked, and the bank has given Dell Duke the go-ahead to do the garden conversion.

But the letter (which is from the senior vice president's office) has additional information besides the legal permission to take up the rock pile.

Someone over there at North South Bank is on top of things, because as the letter states:

> Taking the initiative to improve the
> property as a renter shows a commitment
> to the values we at North South Bank
> hold dear.
>
> We have never, in the history of the
> bank, seen such a thorough proposal.
>
> Therefore, Mr. Duke, in addition to
> granting you permission to plant a gar-
> den in the central, uncovered atrium, we
> have made the decision to ask you to be
> the Building Representative for the Gar-
> dens of Glenwood.

I don't think anyone ever asked Dell to represent anything before.

He looks like he won the lottery.

It's a strange combination of being wildly excited and deeply afraid.

I'm wondering now about his parents.

Maybe as a toddler he was locked in a woodshed in a cold climate for extended periods of time.

He appears to have just been let out.

Looking at him as he reads the letter a sixth time aloud, I realize he's sort of weeping.

I assure him that being the building rep is a big honor that he richly deserves.

The next thing I know, he's down in the garage putting a sign in front of the best parking space in the open carport.

It reads:

RESERVED FOR BUILDING REP

DELL DUKE: UNIT 28

I guess he just doesn't get what being of service means.

Now that we have permission, the plan can be executed.

It's Saturday, and we're all here except Pattie, who has the most customers on the weekends.

I ask Quang-ha how he would suggest we remove the

red lava rock. I'm secretly thinking he might want to get involved in all of this.

He isn't remotely interested.

But apparently he got something out of *Tom Sawyer,* even if he didn't read it or write the paper on Mark Twain.

He only says:

"Give the rock away. People love anything they think is free."

This strikes me as accurate.

I go down the hall to discuss the idea with Dell. Sadhu is there in the living room.

He's a lot nicer to me since I made Dell a computer. He has even asked my opinion on a few technical things.

And I'm allowed to borrow his fifteen-watt soldering gun.

When I explain to Dell that my plan is to give away the rock, Sadhu says:

"List it online. It will be gone before you know it."

I post an offering of free red lava landscaping rock.

I say that if you can haul it away, you can have it.

Only 7 minutes later, I get my first response.

Quang-ha appears to be right.

The idea of something for nothing is appealing in some visceral way.

Even if free things are never free.

The burden of ownership means everything has a price.

I think that's why really rich and famous people look so weighed down and glum in most photos.

They know that they have to keep their guard up. They have things other people want.

I have said that the red rock is on a first come, first serve basis.

Before I know what's going on, I have four different people over here fighting over the stuff.

The lava rock enthusiasts scare me.

Since Dell is now the building rep, I make him go down and deal with it.

I have no idea what he says, but Mai and I hear all kinds of shouting.

The important thing is that in two hours all of the rock is gone, and so is the ripped black plastic sheeting underneath.

I said that it was also free.

We all head downstairs (even Quang-ha wants a look) and we stare at the newly exposed dirt.

What remains is only the hard-packed ground. It's not even brown. It's dusty gray.

Maybe the construction crew dumped a few leftover bags of concrete on their way out.

I guess everyone is thinking the same thing, but Quang-ha is always the one who gives the unspoken a voice.

He says:

"Nothing's going to grow here."

Pattie has just come home from work and she seems more worn out than usual. She stands with us and stares at the big rectangle of nothing. Finally she adds:

"It's a bigger-looking space when it's not covered with rocks."

Dell chimes in:

"And a bigger project than anyone thought."

Pattie sighs and starts up the stairs.

"Most things are."

I don't want to be crushed, but it's possible they are talking about me, not the ugly, exposed area that is now the centerpiece of the courtyard.

Mai puts her hand on my shoulder. She says:

"Let's go eat. Everything looks better in the daylight."

It looks even worse in the full sun.

I go downstairs early, and it's only me and the dirt, which I now realize has a gritty top, like someone sprinkled coarse sea salt on a gray cracker.

Even if I got everyone in this entire complex to join me here with garden tools, I don't think we could make it happen.

Plus I've only seen a few of the other residents. And they don't look like people who would want to swing a pickaxe.

Regular soil is a crazy mix of everything from fine rock fragments to water, air, insects, and even bacteria and fungi.

It's all necessary.

I remember the first time I looked under the microscope at a pinch of the dirt from my own backyard.

It was a shocker.

Now, as I think about this open space, I know what has to be done.

Deep tilling of the soil isn't a good idea unless you are facing the kind of ground we have here in the Gardens of Glenwood.

But this situation calls for heavy machinery.

We have to rent a Rototiller.

I can't do this myself for all kinds of reasons, not the least of which is that you have to be eighteen years old to even legally operate the equipment.

I go back upstairs, and when Mai wakes up, I explain the situation.

She doesn't look like she has any idea what I'm talking about, even when I clarify that a Rototiller is a machine with sharp blades that mechanically chop soil.

But she understands something, because she says:

"So we need an adult, a credit card, and a car?"

Dell wants no part of this.

Mai has done a lot of talking, but it's the resident from unit #11 who makes the difference.

A guy named Otto Sayas—I would give anything to have a name that was a palindrome—knocks on the door.

He wants to know what's happening with the "big dirt patch in the courtyard."

Otto Sayas doesn't look very happy, because his unit opens right up onto the future garden site.

I'm guessing from his attitude that he didn't have a problem with the patch of red lava rock and weeds.

Dell has to talk to the guy because he's the building rep. I hear him explain:

"It's all going to be planted. You'll see. We are right in the middle of the project."

I catch sight of Otto Sayas and he's still scowling. He barks:

"Nothing in the world will grow there."

Then the magical part happens, because Dell sort of puffs up and says:

"You just wait and see."

chapter 49

A Rototiller is like a jackhammer, but for dirt. And we get one.

Quang-ha doesn't come to Sam's U-Rent on Saturday because he is going bowling.

I had no idea he was a bowler.

But maybe that's how it is with bowling. You do it and then leave it behind.

I think Dell would have liked to go bowling instead of to Sam's U-Rent.

But he's agreed to this.

The machine we rent requires real upper body strength to operate, especially when it is attacking hard ground.

So only Dell can use it.

Dell's pretty doughy around the middle, and his large stomach vibrates as if it's been put in a can and shaken at the paint store in one of those mixing machines.

But the good news is that the solid ground really gets pulverized.

The bad news is that Dell is probably going to be too sore to walk for a week.

I investigate the newly tilled soil downstairs in the future garden.

At dinner I share the good news:

"I tested the soil. And it is neutral. The pH is a perfect 7."

Mai and Pattie and Dell look up from their food. Quang-ha keeps shoveling with his fork.

Plants (like people) thrive when there is balance.

So when the soil is too acidic, which can be thought of as sour, you should lower the pH factor.

You can do this by adding lime.

When the soil is too alkaline, which can be thought of as being too sweet, you need to add sulfur.

I explain this, but I can tell that it's not a spellbinding discussion for the people I live with.

Dell says:

"Did you taste the soil to find out?"

I can't tell whether Dell means this as a joke or not, but it causes Quang-ha to laugh.

I realize that whenever he laughs it's some kind of relief.

It's like a dam bursting.

Pattie says:

"That's great, Willow."

Quang-ha then mutters:

"What's really being measured are ions of hydrogen."

He seems as surprised as I am at his own statement. He puts more spicy sauce on his pork, looking guilty, as if learning something in science class is a crime.

Table silence.

Mai then says:

"And 7 is your favorite number, Willow."

I don't explain that I don't count by 7s anymore, but I do still appreciate the beauty of the number.

I'm thinking that everyone will get more involved tomorrow when we do the planting.

And I find I'm really looking forward to that.

There was an X factor.

An unseen, or unknown, influence.

We went to sleep with a large rectangle of newly tilled, well-balanced soil in the courtyard where we live.

It was a thing of beauty.

At least to me.

But a Santa Ana wind blew in, in the middle of the night. This happens here.

Certain conditions propel a stream of dry air from the mountains to the shoreline.

We wake to a dustbowl.

I have never seen such filth.

The walls and the windows of the first-floor units are covered in a layer of newly ground dirt.

I go downstairs and I stare.

It's as if a grime tornado hit the place.

After I show Dell, he limps to the garage and yanks down the building rep parking sign. He doesn't want anyone to know where he lives.

Dell is so sore from his Rototiller experience that he can barely move.

Or maybe he's just that upset about the dirt damage.

He wraps himself in a blanket, lies down on the floor of his apartment, and closes his eyes. He looks like a mummy.

I would like to take a picture, but I decide it's not appropriate.

Mai has a plan.

She puts up a large sign downstairs. It says:

CONSTRUCTION PROJECT UNDER WAY
APOLOGIES FOR INCONVENIENCE

I feel like we should tell Dell what we're up to, but Mai says to leave him alone.

Mai then gets her mother to drive Dell's car to Sam's U-Rent, where we return the Rototiller and now rent a power sprayer.

Mai and Dell have different approaches to everything in life.

Mai is the ultimate pragmatist. Maybe she gets that from her mother.

Power sprayers are powerful.

Hence the name.

I haven't been around one until now, and so this is all new to me.

We get back to the Gardens of Glenwood and Mai goes upstairs and puts on her new (used) raincoat.

She bought the designer jacket when I got my running shoes and I thought it was a waste of money.

Now I wish I had one.

Quang-ha comes downstairs when we're just about to get started.

Maybe because the rental equipment resembles a machine gun, he looks interested.

Quang-ha wants to try pressure spraying.

He fires up the engine and it's as if he's holding an Uzi.

The force of the water takes a lot of strength to control.

A river of grime falls.

I watch, from a distance, and it takes some time before

I realize something else is happening besides the clean-up.

The pink paint underneath the dirt is also being removed.

And so is the bumpy stucco coating.

This is all demonstrating the theory of connectedness.

Not mathematically speaking, but in a real-world way.

Removing the lava rock and black plastic liner exposed the hard-packed dirt.

Once that was tilled and the wind whipped a portion of it up onto the walls, the power sprayer was brought in, and that started to take off the deadly colored pink paint as well as the grime.

What's underneath is a soft, natural gray.

But now we have to power spray the whole place to make it match.

Or else repaint the building.

Connectedness.

One thing leads to another.

Often in unexpected ways.

chapter 50

We rotate.

If the sprayer is on the lowest setting, even I can manage.

Quang-ha does a huge section, pretending, I believe, that he's in a video game.

I take my turn, but my productivity is lousy.

It's such a struggle for me to control the nozzle that I can barely move.

I am the littlest one, but I give it everything I have. I'm pretty sure that if I hadn't been doing my afternoon jogging, I wouldn't have lasted for more than a minute on my feet.

We have to be very careful because the filthy water runs down the windows. So after we've washed an area, we then need to clean the glass. But we can't do that with the power sprayer.

We are all now working, even Dell, when Jairo's taxi pulls up.

I see him and Pattie talking for a while at the curb.

Somehow, it doesn't seem strange that his whole backseat just happens to be filled with rags and three of those squeegee things.

Jairo finds an extension ladder in the carport and he takes over the window issues.

It's dark and we're still at it.

Even Quang-ha hasn't given up.

We take turns sitting on plastic milk crates and aiming flashlight beams up at the building.

A man comes out and we think he's going to yell at us. But he's friendly and gives us each a peppermint candy.

He even donates a poinsettia for the garden when we're ready to plant. He's had it for almost a year and can't believe he's kept it alive.

We have finished the interior courtyard walls, and now we're working our way around the outside of the building.

We have brooms to direct the run-off, which is a big job in and of itself.

There is a pink-brown stream with stucco bits that flows from whatever area has been sprayed.

If you aren't aiming the light, you are swooshing the water down into the drains.

Jairo has been washing windows for hours.

Quang-ha has taken control as the Most Valuable Player of apartment power spraying.

He is the only one who power sprays like an athlete.

Since I've never seen him do any kind of sport, and I'm skeptical about his bowling, I'm surprised.

Physical stamina is a component in leadership, even in the modern world, where it isn't necessary to be able to harness an ox.

Because it is still impressive if you can.

As it gets really late, Dell retrieves one of his old lawn chairs from the second-floor balcony.

He starts to relax.

Or maybe the muscle pain relievers Pattie gave him kick in.

People now seem to think the garden is a good idea. It's possible they are just thrilled to have their windows washed.

The sky is filled with stars.

More stars than I ever remember seeing, and I've spent a lot of time at night with my head tilted back analyzing the constellations.

Quang-ha has done more laughing in the last ten hours than I've seen in the last ten weeks.

He just finds everything funny now.

I didn't understand until recently that emotions could be so contagious.

I now know why comedians are important in culture.

Sitting on a milk crate in the middle of the night with a flashlight illuminating what at this point is a paint-blasting project, I laugh too.

At nothing, really.

Then I realize that I'm laughing because I'm laughing.

It's after three in the morning.

Jairo's gone. Pattie went to bed after he left. Mai can't seem to stop herself from pushing run-off water away from the building with a broom.

Dell is still outside, but he's been asleep on his lawn chair for an hour. He got cold and climbed into a black plastic garbage bag. He punched his feet through the bottom and now he reminds me of a talking raisin I once saw in a TV commercial.

A guy in the apartments across the street told us to turn off the machine a few hours ago, but Quang-ha ignored him.

Finally, Quang-ha gives us a signal and Mai kills the motor.

She and Quang-ha and I stand back and point our flashlights as we stare at what's been done.

Layers have been removed.

Of dirt.

And pink paint.

And acne-like, lumpy stucco.

The whole surface of the structure is smooth and sleek.

All the cracks are gone. And so are the bald patches where the stucco had crumbled off.

The odd design of the place, with its high windows and box-like mass, now appears futuristic and forward-thinking.

At least to me.

And it is not an exaggeration to say that the Gardens of Glenwood is the cleanest building in all of Bakersfield.

For three days, it is hard for any of us to move our arms.

We walk around like plastic soldiers with our limbs held tightly to our sides.

I go down at night and water the dirt to keep it from blowing again.

And I prep the soil. I add a slow release, granular fertilizer that I got Dell to buy at Home Depot.

By mid-week we are ready for the next step.

We have over four dozen sunflowers, in twenty-three containers, a less-than-thriving poinsettia, and bags of mulch to spread.

As soon as we put the sunflowers in the ground, they should take off.

They will send roots down as far as six feet into the soil. Their single stems in the next few weeks will each produce a terminal flower bud.

I know how this all works.

About a month later, after they've gained up to eight feet in height, the large, flat disk that is the flower will unfurl.

For a week it will bloom.

Bees will arrive and pollinate the many florets that make up what we think of as the single flower (but what is in reality many, many small blossoms).

A week later, when the blooming is over, the florets will turn into seeds, and ripen.

All of the energy will move to this next generation of life.

The plant will have given birth to the future, and then it will be done.

This is the way it works. From the bacteria in the sink to the fruit fly circling the bowl of bananas. We're all doing the same thing.

But if people saw all of this for what it really is, who knows if anyone would get out of bed in the morning?

I will soon have the garden covered with a crop of sunflowers, but in five weeks it will have to be replanted.

And so will I.

What goes in the soil next should be more permanent.

Right now I'm the sunflower.

Temporary, but attaching myself to the ground underneath me.

The garden is challenging me, as always, to see my own situation.

My court hearing is next month.

I'll be ready. I'm not sure for what exactly.

But maybe that's what being ready really means.

chapter 51

⤺

Dell pulled into the parking lot.
There wasn't a place for him, for his car, for his always-now-sore-from-exercising body.

After circling the lot in frustration, he lined up in front of the only available spot he could find.

It was tiny, crowded on one side by a school district van and on the other by the chain-link fence that wrapped around the entire property.

Dell stepped on the gas, intent on inching slowly ahead. Instead, his foot slipped.

Every hair on his body stood on end at the sound of metal on metal as the fencepost dug a crease along the entire right side of his vehicle.

Dell cut the engine as he shouted and swore and pounded his fist (which hurt because he accidentally hit the dashboard instead of the upholstery).

He found himself thinking of Willow. She would have told him before he went forward that the space was too small. She would have calculated the mass or the distance or figured out something.

Dell pushed the thought of the girl out of his mind and opened the door.

He was faced with another harsh reality.

Even though he'd almost taken out the fencing along the passenger's side, he was still so close to the van next to him that he doubted he could get out of his car.

He'd just have to make this work.

Wasn't that what life was now teaching him?

Dell gritted his teeth and got his left leg and then hip out.

But his tummy, even angled and sucked in, was a real problem.

Hoping for the best, he let his belly go. It pushed in all directions, and the edge of his car door dug straight into the side of the neighboring van.

Another metal on metal sound.

He stared wide-eyed at the damage.

That van panel was like cardboard!

Dell slammed his door shut and took off in a run away from the scratched-metal crime scene.

But as he made his way through the rows of cars, a dark mass leaped from behind a tire and slithered right between his wobbly legs.

Dell felt the fur touch his ankles and he shrieked like a startled child.

Inside the low brick building that housed most of the administration, he could see heads suddenly appear in windows.

Dell dropped down to the asphalt to shield himself from the peeping professionals.

And that's when he got a close-up look at the creature formerly known as Cheddar.

The cat was thin and mangy with one hairless ear and a chunk missing from his now-crooked tail.

But the animal was more than scarred and dirty; he was frantic and desperate.

Cheddar arched his back and in an attempt to appear fierce, showed his spiky teeth as his pale green eyes turned dark jade.

A chill ran up Dell's spine.

He had adopted Cheddar, and then he'd let the animal fend for himself in a parking lot.

He had not made a single attempt to rescue him.

Dell stared into the eyes of the frightened feline, and something clicked.

He had to take more responsibility for his actions.

He'd start with the cat.

Dell grabbed Cheddar by the scruff of the neck and was surprised at how easy it was to get control of the animal.

Cheddar was not a feral cat.

He'd been brought up with the touch of a human hand and he seemed perfectly happy to get back in the company of a man with possible access to canned food.

Dell crossed the lot back to his car and then he squeezed himself and Cheddar into his vehicle.

Cheddar jumped into the back as Dell started the engine.

He could hear a new sound now. It was low, but distinct.

The cat was purring under his seat.

Dell reversed out of the parking spot, and curiously this time the fence post didn't even touch his vehicle.

Dell dropped off Cheddar at a vet on Central Avenue with instructions for a flea bath and a full exam. He'd pick the animal up at the end of the day.

He then returned to the school district offices, and this time parked on the street and walked two blocks.

He then went straight to the main office, and reported damaging the van.

It turned out the school district had insurance and the woman told him not to worry.

Dell went to his office with a spring in his step.

Maybe it was the running. He'd lost almost fifteen pounds.

Or maybe it was knowing that he'd done right by Cheddar.

chapter 52

The cat is back.

It's very big news around here.

At least to me.

Sadhu is allergic, so Cheddar is going to live with us in #28.

For now.

I'm obsessed with this cat.

And it's working out because Cheddar is sort of obsessed with me, or at least very interested, which in the world of felines counts as obsessive behavior.

The cat sleeps on my bunk of the Semper Fi beds, tucked inside the curl of my body.

He wheezes once he's really asleep.

When I get up early to go to the bathroom I see the cat move his crooked tail in his sleep.

His paws twitch.

He's running.

I would like to see those dreams.

Cheddar waits on the ledge of the front window for me to come home from the salon in the afternoon.

Or maybe he just enjoys the view. But it certainly looks like he sits with a sense of expectation.

I have my life's savings in a metal box under my bed.

I have tried to contribute each week for food costs (I think of it as a reverse allowance), but Pattie refuses to accept the money.

I try to get Dell to take some and he also says no. His no isn't as solid as her no, but he gets his point across.

So today is the first time I'm spending any of my cash.

I go to the pet store on 7th Street.

I pick out a lime-green breakaway safety cat collar. It is highly reflective and glows in the dark.

I pay an extra two dollars to have *Cheddar* seared into the bendable plastic. I add Pattie's phone number—not Dell's—for emergencies.

I also insist that the collar have a bell. Cats in the wild do so much destruction to the bird population.

But I think that if Cheddar has his way, the cat will never set foot on anything but carpet for the rest of his life.

I've left the door open and he has no interest in even investigating the hallway in our building.

Once I get back to the apartment and Cheddar has

been outfitted with the new collar, Quang-ha complains about what he calls "the annoying ringing."

But even he has to admit that the cat (with the hairless ear and the crooked tail) is in his own way sort of inspiring.

Dell and I talk about practical things now in my weekly sessions.

I have two concerns.

I am anxious, of course, about finding a legal guardian.

And I'm constantly thinking about what to do once the sunflowers are finished.

The plants have grown in these last few weeks and they have bloomed.

Quang-ha's is the tallest. It reached almost seven feet. I think everyone in the building has really appreciated the spectacle.

A few people have complained about the bees.

But it's impossible to please everyone.

Now these plants are on the downside of their lifecycle. I need to think of what to do once they are removed.

If you slice off part of most established plants—this mature plant can be thought of as the parent—and you nurture this severed portion, it will grow.

It is called a cutting.

I have no real resources (that I can think of, because my life's savings don't add up to much) to landscape the large area of soil in the courtyard.

I told the bank that we had a plan, and I presented that in the drawings that were submitted.

But that was hypothetical.

And this is reality.

I'm going to need to take life from what I can find in the neighborhood around me in Bakersfield to landscape this place.

I start small.

A basket.

Scissors.

Wet paper towels (to keep my clippings moist).

I have a few small cuttings taking root in water glasses by the window.

I need to think bigger.

Dell drives me to the Southside plant nursery on Saturday and we buy rooting hormone and three large bags of potting soil.

While we're there, I see Henry E. Pollack. He runs the place.

I have known this guy since I was very young.

He and my dad used to talk about football and he gave us discounts for years.

I've looked at fungus and insect infestation for him in the past.

And I've given advice on grafting limbs on fruit trees.

I'm in the back checking out their new pittosporum tenuifolium, and I catch sight of Dell talking to Henry in the corner.

It looks sort of serious, which makes me nervous.

In the car, I ask Dell what they were whispering about and he says:

"Henry wanted to know how you were doing."

People are uncomfortable asking a kid that question. So they ask adults.

But those adults a lot of times have no clue about the answer.

I look out the window at all the plants growing in people's gardens, and get lost in that.

But later, at the stoplight, I say:

"I'm trying not to put down permanent roots. That's probably what you should tell people like Henry."

Quang-ha is on the couch watching a TV show about a guy who drives around the country in a convertible eating bacon cheeseburgers.

Mai is looking at a catalog for swimsuit enthusiasts.

Dell is clipping his beard into a paper bag (to keep the bits from flying around the room).

Cheddar is asleep.

Pattie is at the salon.

She has been staying late more often now. I worry about that, but she doesn't like anyone to question her schedule.

I come into the living room and explain my plan, which is for us to drive around town and take small cuttings from interesting plants.

Quang-ha doesn't look at me but manages to say:

"Would that be stealing?"

I'm encouraged. At least I have his attention.

"This is an interesting question. If we were on someone's private property, we would be trespassing. And that's breaking the law."

Quang-ha then mumbles something that I can't understand.

So I continue:

"Plants are people's property. But what if the plant extends into the area of the sidewalk? What if we are on public property, such as a park or a library or a state building?"

Quang-ha keeps his eyes on the television and says:

"What if you move to the left? You're blocking part of the TV."

I take a step to the side.

Silence.

Only the television and the sounds of Dell struggling to clip his shockingly wiry facial hair.

And then Quang-ha says:

"Just take stuff out of people's green trash cans. The work will already be done for you."

I look at him now with admiration.

Quang-ha's mother is the hardest worker that I've ever seen. And she has passed on to her son a unique quality. He understands labor in a different way.

If he's not interested in something, he will do anything to get out of doing it.

I mean it when I say to him:

"Quang-ha, you may very well have a future career in management."

As if to drive home his point he says:

"If there are any ice-cream bars in the freezer, I'll take one."

There have never been ice-cream bars in the freezer, but I now will buy a box at the first opportunity.

chapter 53

⟨∾⟩

For the next 17 days, Mai, Dell, and I become experts in the green garden trash cans.

In our town, trash is separated, with blue cans for recycling and green for anything from the yard. Black is for everything else.

My first observation: The green receptacles are not always filled with just cut grass and dead flowers.

I've found spaghetti in there. And all kinds of other objectionable things.

Some of them beyond creepy.

But for the most part, the people of Bakersfield, California, are following the rules of rubbish, meaning that they are tossing their garden waste in the right direction.

And this stuff is mostly alive.

Pattie doesn't want any more tubs or containers in the apartment. She put her foot down on that. And Dell only has his room down the hall, where Sadhu has strict rules.

Again, Quang-ha is the one who has the answer.

"Take everything up to the roof. No one goes up there."

He hasn't been back since we put the broken glass on the skylight, but he obviously remembers what a wide-open space it is.

So now there are pots and containers all over the flat space.

With the rooting hormone and so much full sun and water, I've got a mini-nursery going.

And then we lose almost all of the plants.

There is a light rain and someone named S. Godchaux in unit #21 reports a small leak in the ceiling in his bathroom.

He calls the bank, and they don't notify the building rep. They notify their repairman.

Pattie and I are at the salon and of course I know nothing about this until it is all too late.

A roofer comes and can't make heads or tails out of the containers with the cuttings.

To him, it just looks like a big mess that is getting in the way of an area he needs to tar.

He gets back in touch with the bank, and apparently

someone named Chad Dewey says that nothing should be up there.

So the workers gather all the plants that are growing (or at least trying to form roots), and carry them downstairs, where they are deposited in the Dumpster.

I come home to the crime scene.

Today the city picked up the trash.

I have to piece together the sequence of events, and when I get to the bottom of it, I believe that the plant loss is not just a defeat; it's a sign.

I'm not really going to live at the Gardens of Glenwood for much longer.

Very soon I'm going to be placed in a foster home.

I'm going to be sent back to school.

What's going on here will end.

For me at least.

When I go see Dell for counseling the next day, I tell him:

"I can't return to the past. Having a garden in the courtyard will not ever be the same as what was in my backyard at home."

Dell only nods. And looks sweaty.

Later I see Dell hand Mai an envelope when he comes

over for dinner. And then when I go to bed, I find the note on my pillow. It reads:

Willow—
When they find the place for you (and it will be a great place and it will be right for you, I know that) I want you to try to take Cheddar with you. I will call Lenore and say that the cat is a therapy dog.

Yours in friendship,
Dell Duke

He said that the cat was a therapy dog.

I appreciate his support, but I sincerely hope that he's not running this show.

Two days pass and instead of taking the bus home from the nail salon, I go to Southside nursery.

I find Henry and I explain about the sunflowers and losing my clippings and I ask for advice.

He has to go into the back because a truck is delivering something.

I wait.

There are cartons of ladybugs for sale on the counter and I decide to buy one.

They are usually burnt orange, but as I peer through

the mesh that covers the container, the little bugs moving around in curls of wood look bright red.

I know what Pattie would say.

Lucky.

And she would be right because only a few minutes later Henry comes back in and says he's going to help me. He'll stop by after work and take a look at what I've got going on.

I feel relieved.

Which feels strange.

I walk back to the Gardens of Glenwood and I try to move in a very careful way because I don't want to jiggle the ladybugs.

When I come through the door Quang-ha, who is on the couch as usual, sees the container in my hands and says:

"Did you bring home food?"

I say:

"I brought home insects."

But I smile and I don't even realize it until I catch sight of myself in the mirror.

I'm surprised.

I look different when I smile.

Maybe everyone does.

I don't go to the nail salon this morning.

I stay back to wait for the plant delivery.

Henry came yesterday and took a look. He said he'd bring me some things.

But it's not just the regular nursery van that arrives at 10:07 A.M.

What pulls up is a large truck. And there is a forklift in the back. A van follows with four workers.

I go out to the street, and Henry and his cousin Phil are just lowering the lift-gate.

In the truck I see a big box of timber bamboo. It is being transported on its side. Standing upright, it would be over twenty feet tall.

There are other plants in the truck:

Pink stripe phormium.

A diverse selection of flowering vines (to climb up the metal poles to the second story).

Ground cover.

Even a three-year-old cherry tree.

I am overwhelmed.

But there isn't time to express it because there is a lot to be done.

The four workers cut down the sunflowers.

This would have been sad except that it isn't now.

We decide to hang the long stalks from the second-floor balcony. The large flowers are the size of human heads. The bright yellow petals are now dried and the centers are dark.

Henry has green twine and I'm in charge of that project while down below, the workers dig a huge hole because this bamboo they brought is serious business.

While I'm tying the sunflower stalks to the railing, Henry comes to tell me that this is all a gift.

I try to say thank you, but the words are stuck.

My mouth is open and I'm suddenly some kind of fish out of water. You can't see the hook, but it must be in my cheek.

Or maybe it's in my heart, because that's being pulled.

Henry puts his arm around my shoulder and whispers: "You're welcome."

It takes almost four hours to plant all of the stuff.

But the day is not over.

As another surprise, Lorenzo from Bakersfield Electric brings a set of solar-powered lights, which at night will send shafts up through the foliage into the starry sky.

It is all so much more than I hoped for.

Lorenzo says that the nursery guys called him. He explains about something called the "favor bank."

I haven't heard about this before, but I'm thinking that I have a lot of accounts with people at this point.

I watch as Lorenzo puts the light fixtures in place, but I can't stop myself and end up moving them around so that they are just where I think they should be.

I explain that I like to see space in terms of triangles, and he listens for a while and then laughs.

When we finish, he gives me his card and says he wants to talk to me about a big lighting job he's bidding on at the new shopping complex.

I tell him I'd be glad to look at his design sketches.

It can be part of my favor bank.

After he's gone, I water everything with a hose Henry left for me.

I'm just finishing when Mai comes down the sidewalk.

I go out through the gate and she follows me inside, and I wish that Henry and Phil and Lorenzo and the guys had all stayed.

They deserve to see the look on her face.

We sit on the stairs and watch as people arrive home.

Everyone is pretty much stunned.

I decide not to run my mile, so I'm here when Quang-ha comes in.

He doesn't say a single word.

I wait. He's still silent as he takes a seat next to me on the stairs.

More silence.

Then he turns and says:

"I don't want to know how you did it. I want to believe that you're magic."

Maybe because he's older and a boy, and maybe because he wasn't really on board with me coming to stay with them, I feel something wash over me when I hear the words.

I think the feeling is acceptance.

The three of us are all together on the steps when Dell comes in from the carport.

I guess he knew something was going to happen. He says that Henry called him. I can't believe he was able to keep any kind of secret.

Dell is very, very happy when he sees the plants.

Mai uses Dell's cell phone to tell her mom to come home early. She wants her to get a view of this garden in the daylight.

Pattie makes it to the apartment just as the horizon is going purple.

There are streaks of color overhead as she looks up into the darkening sky.

She says:

"It is no longer wrong to call this place the Gardens of Glenwood."

We go upstairs together and I take Cheddar and lie down on my bed.

I'm exhausted.

So is Cheddar, I think, but snoozing is his default setting, so I can't be sure.

I fall asleep even though I haven't eaten dinner and it's barely dark outside. I wake up to the sound of the television and the smell of popcorn.

Quang-ha appears in the doorway and says:

"Dell put up the 'building rep' sign again in front of the best parking spot."

We look right at each other.

We are laughing, but with our eyes.

chapter 54

⟨∽⟩

D ell got the mail.
It was always bad news, so sometimes days went by
before he bothered to take out his strangely sharp little
key and open the metal box by the front gate.

The mailbox was stuffed.

As always, there were overdue bills mixed with throw-
away flyers printed with cheap black ink that rubbed off
onto his fingers.

But today there was something more.

He held a letter addressed to Pattie Nguyen in his
hands.

She didn't get mail here. He read the return address.

KERN COUNTY DEPARTMENT OF CHILD SERVICES

And he felt suddenly queasy.

He was sweating and dizzy.

Maybe he should just leave.

He could drive off and never come back.

If he did, at least the cat would be covered. He couldn't
imagine a world where Willow wouldn't figure out a place
for the furball.

Dell had delivered the letter to Pattie. And then he'd gone straight down the hall to his room.

Now he was in bed and his laptop was open. He was staring at the Kern County Child Services website.

In the state of California, a person could have temporary custody of a ward of the state for a few weeks, or under special circumstances, for several months.

But after that, the goal was for permanency. The hope was that a guardian would step forward.

Dell felt his left leg twitch.

And then it jerked, spontaneously, like he was kicking a soccer ball.

Ever since he'd started jogging, his limbs seemed to function independently from the rest of his body.

Now, even lying down, it was as if his feet were trying to step forward.

Was it possible he could become the guardian of a twelve-year-old?

Even if he wanted to (and he didn't really, did he?), he had debt and barely any job security and he'd never even been able to follow through on getting his coffee card stamped correctly at the little place where he sometimes got a morning cup of hot brew.

But hadn't things changed?

Wasn't he now the building rep for the Gardens of Glenwood?

Hadn't he been driving the two Nguyen kids to school every day?

Plus, he wasn't just holding down a job; he was possibly getting better at it.

Wasn't he the one who supervised the biggest transformation that had ever happened at the apartment building?

Okay, so maybe he hadn't supervised, but he was at least a part of it. He did operate the Rototiller.

Dell shut his laptop.

But his legs kept twitching.

⁖⁖⁖

No one knew that they had gotten close.

And now Jairo was the first person Pattie needed to talk to.

His cell phone rang but he didn't answer. She knew that if he was driving, he couldn't pick up.

But he would. He'd call her back and they would figure out—the two of them—what to do.

It was December, and the brutal heat that was the only real constant for months had finally broken the week before. It was like someone flipped a switch and changed the season.

Nights were now suddenly cool, and fans and air conditioners had finally been put away for their four-month-long electronic hibernation.

Pattie slipped out of her too-tight shoes (her feet seemed to be growing) and stared at the letter from the state of California.

It was for the custody hearing.

It had twice been postponed.

Now it was for real.

Decisions had to be made.

She folded the letter in half and promised herself that she'd do the right thing.

chapter 55

❧

As we are climbing into the bunk beds, I explain to Mai that everything is in shock, which happens when a plant is first put down into new soil.

I know from experience that some things will thrive and others will wither.

Only time will expose the difference.

Balance is critical in the natural world.

I'm still feeling the triumph of the garden the next day when I get the news.

I don't like Lenore Cole from Jamison, but in the name of fairness, I admit it would be hard to build a case that she isn't doing her job.

She has found a place for me.

It's permanent.

She has come over today to the nail salon to tell me in person. She then asks me if there is anything that I need.

We've been speaking outside in the parking lot, but Pattie must know.

I have been with them for almost three months.

It was always temporary.

Pattie had never met me until the day a hospital supply truck drove through a red light.

I understand better than anybody how much she's done for me.

These are the facts.

I'm going to be placed in a group foster care home on 7th Street.

It figures that it wouldn't be Eighth Street or Ninth Street.

She says it's okay for me to cry.

I tell her that I'm fine.

I say that I would like to go to the library, and she volunteers to take me.

I'd like to be around books.

When Lenore and I are ready to leave, Pattie tells me that Dell will pick me up at the library after work.

I won't have to take the bus.

I say thank you and we go to Lenore's car.

I feel numb.

But I'm moving on.

That's how Lenore puts it when we get into her car. Her exact words are:

"It's time to move on."

It feels like something I might hear in a cafeteria lunch

line when I've stared too long at a mysterious noodle dish.

And then Lenore adds:

"Transitions are important. We want you to spend the morning at Jamison tomorrow and then go to the hearing in the afternoon."

So that's moving on.

It means this is happening right away.

This surprises me.

I thought when she told me, she meant in five days or two weeks.

Not tomorrow.

Lenore is a professional and she must have some experience in all of this.

It might be like ripping off a Band-Aid quickly.

It doesn't hurt as much because a large component in pain has to do with anticipation.

So maybe that's why she didn't tell me until now.

I say good-bye to Lenore and go into the library.

Once I get inside, I hold my hands right up close to my face.

I'm breathing too fast. But I'm not crying.

I'm thinking about Mai and Quang-ha and Pattie and Dell.

They are taking me away from these people.

And I don't think I can live now without them.

I go straight to my favorite area, which is upstairs in the corner next to the window.

The light floods this spot.

I get a book on astrophysics. I haven't thought of big-picture concepts in a long time.

Maybe I've been too focused on the smaller things. I've had my mind wrapped around specifics.

Reading about galaxies and cosmic microwaves helps me to breathe more easily.

I'm putting my place in the universe into perspective.

I'm stardust.

I'm golden brown.

I'm just one small bit in a vast expanse.

When the time is right, I go sit outside on the steps.

I think about the Nguyens.

Will they move out of the Gardens? Will Dell go back to #28? Maybe they can rent another apartment and stay in the complex.

Mai won't miss just me; she's going to really miss the bunk beds and the closet.

And what about Cheddar?

If they stay, I can come visit on weekends.

I could still help with the garden.

I could walk, or even call Jairo to drive me over in his taxi.

I could increase my running and plot out a new loop that takes me right by the Gardens of Glenwood.

Dell suddenly appears.

I didn't see him coming. Did he sneak up on me or am I not seeing things now?

He sits down next to me.

But he doesn't say anything.

Then he puts his head between his knees and starts to cry.

It sounds like he's choking to death.

I'm right next to him, and I do what my mother would have done.

I put my arm around his shoulder and softly whisper: "I'm all right. It's going to be okay."

And that breaks him completely.

He cries harder.

He lifts his face and looks at me. I still have my arm encircling his hunched back.

But I see something in his eyes.

He looks heartbroken.

I know the look.

chapter 56

Pattie closed the nail salon early and took the bus home.

It was cloudy outside and the wind was blowing hard down the valley. There was dust and sand in the air, and when her teeth met she felt the grit.

She could taste it when she swallowed.

Pattie came through the door of the apartment and saw Quang-ha at the table doing his homework.

He was never at the table doing his homework.

He was always watching TV.

But he barely looked up as she came in.

He didn't say a thing.

Pattie noticed that his foot was twitching. Back and forth. Not shaking, but close.

She looked down the hall.

Mai was in her room on the upper bunk bed. She had her face close to the wall and the cat held tight to her chest.

So they knew.

Pattie went down the hall and stood in the doorway.

"We're going to figure it all out."

She walked to the bed and put her hand on her daughter's silky head of hair.

"It's temporary."

Suddenly Quang-ha's voice could be heard. He was loud.

"That's what you say about everything. Temporary. Well, if you do something long enough, you don't get to use that word anymore."

Pattie went back to the living room and stood in front of her son. Mai appeared behind her.

Quang-ha looked up at both of them. His eyes were large and defiant.

But his voice was like a small boy's, not a teenage kid's.

"We shouldn't let her go."

Pattie put her arm around her son and they stayed that way for a long time.

Mai came over and leaned against them.

Outside, the gusts picked up. A window was open in the kitchen and they could hear a sound. It was different. It was something new to add to the mix of street noise and people.

It was the bamboo in the new garden.

They could hear the rustling of a thousand leaves.

Dell woke in the middle of the night.

He tried to get back to sleep but tossed and turned so many times it started to feel like exercise.

At 2:47 he was worn out, but still wide-awake, so he got up.

He stayed in his sweatpants and T-shirt, but pulled on his shoes and a windbreaker.

He then went downstairs to the courtyard.

It was cold out and he could see his breath as he made his way to the coiled green hose.

Standing in the light of a partial moon, he watched the water come out in gushes of icy silver.

And even though he was freezing cold, Dell took his time watering Willow's new garden.

The honeysuckle vines were taller than him now, and as he looked them over, he realized that one of the buds was beginning to open.

He knew for certain that it would be magnificent.

chapter 57

❦

I open my eyes. I can hear Mai's soft breathing above me in the bunk bed, but otherwise the apartment is silent.

That's unusual. The world of Pattie Nguyen is always noisy.

Meals are always being cooked, dishes washed, the vacuum or shower running.

But not now.

Because it's really early.

Dell took me to dinner last night to Happy Greens, which is a vegetarian restaurant.

He was trying to cheer me up.

He told me that they were working on some kind of arrangement.

When we got back to the Gardens, I did my best to look happy.

I look at the clock. It is 4:27 A.M.

Quang-ha is asleep on the couch.

The shades in the living room are drawn on the two windows facing the street.

The full moon is right above the skylight and the glow is enough to cast little shadows on the carpet.

In the past I saw these shapes as hopeful.

Now they appear to be stains.

I take my pillow and the fuzzy blanket from my bed and I go sit in the bathroom.

A few minutes later, Cheddar slinks in. He curls up on the edge of the blanket and falls asleep leaning against my back.

There is a window in here, and from my position in the corner on the cold tiles I watch the sunrise bathe the world in orange light.

Stars littering an endless Bakersfield sky begin to dim.

I close my eyes.

And finally, as I drift back to sleep, the screen of my mind fills with hummingbirds.

They understand the importance of motion.

I wake up a few hours later and have no idea where I am.

It takes a moment (which feels like eternity but is in reality less than a second) to process that I'm in the bathroom, and that I won't live at the Gardens of Glenwood after today.

That's the thing about time.

A second can feel like forever if what follows is heart-break.

I am very, very tired, but I take a shower and wash my hair.

I let it dry the way it wants to, which is in a mass of dark curls.

I'm not pulling it back or putting it in a braid or getting it under control.

It is what it is.

I am what I am.

I put on my old gardening outfit.

I put the acorn that Mai gave me into my pocket.

Maybe it will be lucky. I've gotten this far. That says something.

I'm not going to wear my red hat, because I'll be indoors.

But I will carry it with me because red is a lucky color, and very important in the natural world.

It is business as usual at breakfast.

I take a banana, which is covered in brown spots.

It looks like the skin of a giraffe.

I wish that I were old enough to just go live in the Amazon and study the plants there, because it is possible that one of them holds the key to the cure for cancer.

But the obstacles are insurmountable.

I don't even have a passport.

We are trying to eat when Dell comes down the hall earlier than usual.

He and Pattie say they are getting something from the car and they go to the carport.

I'm certain that they are talking about my situation.

They come back up after a few minutes and only say that we have to leave or Mai will be late for the first bell.

I ask Pattie what will happen at the hearing.

She says that I shouldn't worry.

I don't think this is much of an answer.

Who wouldn't be worried?

But what's worse is I know her now. I spend a big part of every day with her. And so I can see by the expression on her face that she's worried too.

Mai wants to go to the hearing in the courthouse this afternoon.

I say to her:

"You don't have to be there. You're supposed to be in school. I'm ready for this now. I'm stronger."

And then I get up and go to the bathroom.

Only minutes later, Lenore arrives.

Pattie says that this isn't good-bye.

It's *Hẹn gặp lại sau.*

That means "see you later."

I say:

"Yes. I will see you all later."

I've got to get out of here before there is too much drama.

I hug Mai and I try to be brave, mostly because she's falling apart for the two of us.

She's always the toughest person in the room, but with me leaving, her armor cracks.

I hug Dell and then I hug Pattie. I give Quang-ha a nod.

Then I turn to Cheddar.

He's sitting on the back of the couch and he's watching. I was going to go say good-bye to him. That was my plan. But now I can't do that.

I turn away.

And I hear the bell on his collar ring.

The only thing I can think to say is:

"Please water the plants in the courtyard. Especially the pittosporum. I'll be over to check on the garden as soon as I can."

I hear Mai heading out of the room, moving down the hallway. She can't take it.

I turn back just before I leave the apartment. Cheddar is under the speckles of colored light from the broken glass on the rooftop.

It makes his face all wobbly.

Or maybe it's just what he looks like through tears.

I climb into Lenore's car and I look up at the building.

I see Cheddar now in the window.

I whisper:

"Good-bye."

I did not say good-bye to my mom or my dad. I never got to do that. They were here and then they were gone.

Does saying good-bye matter?

Does it really end something?

I didn't hug them that morning when I left to go to school.

That's why I don't want to go back there.

I can handle the other kids and the teachers and everything about it but the memory.

I can't be in that place, because every time I allow myself to think about my last day there, I fall apart. I break loose from this world.

I fly into a million pieces.

I am worried about Quang-ha.

I know that he has lots of homework this week. I hope that he at least attempts to do some of it.

And then there is Dell. Will he go back to putting things in closets? Will he return to staring out the window and waiting for his life to begin?

Will Pattie keep working so hard? I know for a fact that those fumes from the nail polish are bad for her.

I realize now that I'm worrying about all of them.

It's better than worrying about myself.

This is one of the secrets that I have learned in the last few months.

When you care about other people, it takes the spotlight off your own drama.

chapter 58

⟨⤳⟩

I'm in a large room with five other girls at Jamison.
We all have hearings today.

Four of the five girls are sleeping. Or at least pretending to.

The fifth girl is talking on a cell phone.

I have my computer with me, and after I ask three times, the woman at the front desk gives me the wireless password.

No one else has a computer. I feel bad using mine, but the other girls don't seem to care.

Everyone in this room is in her own bubble of unhappiness, and there's not a lot of sharing.

I'm grateful for that.

Since I have access to the wireless code, I decide to take a look at the Jamison system.

This system is of course protected, but the firewall isn't very secure. I've looked at a lot of code for electronic buffering.

It's not a very sophisticated network, because I see the

transport layer and recognize it immediately as something I've gotten through.

I'm thinking that not many hacker kids end up here.

I'm not a hacker kid, but I have potential in this area.

I get in right away.

I go to Lenore's account.

When I look at her e-mail, I suddenly feel sorry for her.

She appears to be massively overworked. There is e-mail from juvenile court, from schools, from the police department.

Mountains of the stuff.

I see references to all kinds of medical documents. There are reports of physical abuse and criminal behavior.

I feel sick now.

In a new way.

I really shouldn't be reading these things.

It's all too personal and it's not about me and what I'm doing is wrong.

I have Dell's work files on my computer.

I transferred everything when I put together his laptop, but I never actually looked at any of the stuff.

Now I open one of his files called DDSS. And I read:

```
Dell Duke System of the Strange
1 = MISFIT
2 = ODDBALL
3 = LONE WOLF
4 = WEIRDO
5 = GENIUS
6 = DICTATOR
7 = MUTANT
```

There are many names in most of the categories.

I go through them.

Quang-ha is a lone wolf. And Pattie is a dictator. I see that Mai is a junior dictator.

Then I see that for MUTANT there is only one name.

Dell Duke has listed himself.

At first, I'm appalled.

But then I realize he's only trying to make sense of the world.

He's looking for a way to put things in categories.

He's seeing people as different species.

Of course, he's wrong.

All of us are all of those things. I'm no genius. I'm as much of a lone wolf or a misfit or a weirdo as anyone.

When it came to the garden, I was a dictator.

If there is anything I've figured out in the last months it's that you can find labels to organize living things, but you can't put people in any kind of group or order.

It just doesn't work that way.

I close my computer, and in only a handful of minutes a woman comes into the room to tell us that lunch is being served.

I'm not hungry, but I follow the group to the dining area.

They don't have much of a selection for vegetarians, but I pick my way through a salad and some spinach with alarmingly bright orange-colored cheese sauce.

At least I think it's cheese sauce.

It seems better not to ask.

Everyone else sitting at my table is having a hot dog.

When we are finished they bring us each a bowl of vanilla ice cream with sprinkles on top.

The girl next to me starts to cry when she sees the sprinkles.

I'm wondering if she's worried about the long-term side effects of consuming artificial food coloring.

It's a valid concern.

But I decide she's not crying about that, because she has a horrible burn on her arm and she picks at it as she weeps.

The burn is the size of a cherry.

I get a bad feeling in my stomach thinking that someone did this to her.

Maybe that's even why she's here.

I shut my eyes and do my best to imagine I'm back in the new garden.

And before I know it, my ice-cream bowl looks like soup.

And the colored sprinkles have all sunk.

Lenore comes to get me. She says that she likes the way my hair looks today.

It hasn't changed since she picked me up, so she might just be trying to think of something positive to say to me.

But I smile anyway.

I realize that it's a true smile.

I will go forward into the world and do my best to be the daughter that my parents would have wanted me to be.

I'm not brave; it's just that all other choices have been thrown out the window.

Lenore takes me to see the grief counselor (whose
name is Mrs. Bode-Ernst).

Sitting in her office I realize that I'm not afraid.

Of anything.

A N Y M O R E
N N
Y   Y
M   M
O   O
R   R
E   E

Exactly 7 letters.

Just a coincidence.

Not long ago, I had a lot of fear.

Now it feels like there's not a lot left to be afraid about.

Lenore says:

"Today is all just procedure. You will see the judge in
private. He might ask some questions. There is paperwork
to be signed."

Mrs. Bode-Ernst smiles and I understand that she's
thinking this is good news.

Or maybe she is just smiling to be encouraging.

I don't share her optimism.

The grief counselor says:

"The beginning of anything is hard. I know you've been

through a lot. We're going to get you in school. And you'll make all kinds of new friends. Before you know it, you are going to be right back in the swing of things."

I think about telling her that my school experience was never that great, and besides Margaret Z. Buckle, I didn't have close friends until I met Mai and Quang-ha and lived at the Gardens of Glenwood.

But I don't want to upset her.

How could she know that I never had that kind of swing?

Lenore and I return to her car.

She explains that the judge will take legal responsibility for me.

I'm hoping that it will be a woman and a person of color who sees me and understands that I'm different, even Strange (as Dell Duke figured out), but that I still have value.

The court will now call the shots.

I can tell that Lenore feels bad right now.

But none of this is her fault.

I want her to understand.

I want to tell her that I'm sorry. Instead, I reach over and touch her arm.

Just my fingertips.

After that, I don't have to say anything. I can tell she understands.

I go into the girls' bathroom in the courthouse.

I need a few minutes by myself.

The mirror in here is not made of glass.

It's a polyester film coating made with aluminum stretched perfectly flat against a rectangular board.

So you can't break this mirror.

I'm guessing they think that people who end up here don't need any more bad luck.

I open my mouth and stare.

Because my skin is dark, my teeth look very white. They are straight and I think a good size.

But they are permanent teeth.

There's no hiding it.

I shut my eyes.

I can see my always-smiling mother and my strong father.

I hear their words voiced in so many ways, since as early as I can remember, trying to protect me.

Were they too worried about me to look out for themselves?

Or is life so filled with random action that the very notion of caution is futile?

If the last few months have proven anything, it's that I don't need more theory, but rather more experience with reality.

Even though the dose I've received is enough to last a lifetime.

When I see the judge I will try to convey a positive attitude, while at the same time monitoring my blood pressure and other vital signs.

There have been cases of stress-induced cardiomyopathy, which also is known as broken heart syndrome.

chapter 59

❦

D ell was getting ready.
He picked out a red tie. And put on his suit. It had been the first time he'd told his boss a version of the truth about why he wouldn't be at work.

He was going to juvenile court to be there for one of the kids that he counseled.

Instead of feeling like a lazy slacker, he had thought he could hear admiration in the voice of his supervisor.

Or maybe the guy was just yawning.

Now, as he pulled up the pants on his suit, he was surprised that he was able to button the waistband.

The last time he found himself in this situation he'd used a safety pin to keep the pants closed.

This was solid evidence that he'd been losing weight. Not enough that he could get out of his car when it was pinned up against a van, but still, it felt good to see his stomach receding.

❦

Down the hall in #28, Pattie debated what to wear and settled on a white silk shirt with two embroidered doves.

It came from Vietnam.

She already had on a black skirt from a discount store.

And red slippers.

The doves were a symbol of love.

The black skirt was a show of respect.

And the red slippers were of course lucky.

Probably no one in authority would pick up on the symbolism, but if they did, Pattie wanted to give the right impression of her intent.

⁕

Across town, Mai sat in her high school history class and stared out the window.

It wasn't fair.

She of all people should be there.

She'd started this.

The clock on the far wall behind the teacher's head hadn't moved in what seemed like forever.

The woman was going on and on about ancient Rome when it became clear to Mai that the only thing that mattered was in a courthouse in downtown Bakersfield.

By the time the bell rang, she knew one thing with absolute certainty.

⁕

Mai explained to the woman in the office that there was a family emergency.

And then she used a trick. She started speaking in Vietnamese. Rapid fire.

That unnerved people.

The next thing she knew, she had a permission slip to get Quang-ha out of biology (where he was actually paying attention to a short film on mitosis).

And only minutes later the two Nguyens were walking out the front doors on their way downtown.

Mai looked back at the school and saw a decal in a classroom window.

It was of a sunflower. Bathed in the hard light, it glowed as if it were made of gold.

Mai took that to be a good sign.

chapter 60

F amily court has its own area on the second floor of City Hall.

I could ask a million questions about what will happen next, but I've decided that I'm going to go where the wind takes me.

And it's gusting outside, so if that's any indicator, maybe I'll be blown far.

Lenore knows her way around this place and a lot of people say hello. She keeps her hand on my shoulder, which is a nice touch.

She says that she will be there for me.

I'm taken into a waiting area.

They don't have kids sit in the main room, and that makes sense.

I see a little boy come in and he's crying. He's small. He looks like he's only six or 7 years old.

A man picks him up and whispers in the boy's ear, but he keeps crying.

I'm glad I can't hear what is being said.

I think that waiting is the hardest part.

I'm okay with it, though, because it's not like I'm rushing to get somewhere.

Lenore leaves the room and I realize now that I could run away.

I could just walk out the door and keep going.

But I don't do that. And not just because I'm tired.

I have given in.

But that's different from giving up.

After a long time, a woman appears and says that it's my turn to see the judge.

I don't know what happened to Lenore, and I feel like I should wait for her.

But the woman says that Lenore's dealing with something unexpected.

I just shrug.

I think that everything Lenore deals with is unexpected.

I follow the new woman in charge down the hall, and we turn and enter what is the judge's chamber.

I guess saying judge's *office* doesn't sound as powerful.

And that's when I see them.

They are standing.

Dell has on a suit, which is pretty tight.

Next to him on one side is Quang-ha.

On the other is Pattie.

At Pattie's elbow is Jairo. He also wears a suit, so I almost don't recognize him.

And in front, holding a big bunch of tulips, is Mai.

They are all smiling.

I don't say anything. And I don't move. I am completely still.

I know how to do that.

At the desk, a woman gets to her feet. She is wearing what I guess is a judge's robe, but it looks like a choir outfit. I don't even blink as she says:

"Willow, I'm Judge Biederman. And I think that you know these people."

I'm not sure what to do.

I realize that tears are flooding my eyes, but I'm not crying. I'm just drippy.

I don't know what any of this means.

The judge continues:

"There has been a formal request made today to the court for your guardianship. In a motion filed by Mr. Jairo Hernandez and Ms. Dung Nguyen—"

Pattie interrupts the judge:

"It's Pattie."

Judge Biederman continues, but I don't think people break in on her very often, because her nose wrinkles up.

"Mr. Hernandez and Ms. *Pattie* Nguyen are seeking this custody agreement as partners . . ."

I don't hear anything after that.

I don't need to.

I know that Lenore comes into the room.

And at some point she has her arm around me. I sink into a chair and I bury my face into my red hat and I'm not sure if I'm laughing or crying.

I hear Mai's voice.

"It's going to be all right now. Don't cry, Willow."

I answer in Vietnamese:

"Được hơn là bình thường."

Which means:

"It's more than all right."

Pattie and Jairo aren't getting married or anything like that.

But they are in some kind of a relationship, which looks to me like more than just friends.

We find out that Pattie hasn't been working late all the time.

She and Jairo have been going to dinner and even to a few movies, and once to a poetry reading at Bakersfield College.

We all have the same look on our faces when we hear this piece of news.

Quang-ha (of course) is the one who says:

"Poetry reading? You've got to be kidding me."

Dell wanted to go for guardianship too, but he's pretty much broke—even though I recently put his accounts on autopay to help straighten out some of his finances—so he doesn't qualify.

Jairo has some cash in his account (from his prize), but the real discovery is that Pattie is some kind of hoarder.

While Dell spent years piling up plastic plates, Pattie was stacking *money*.

She hid this from everyone, but now that the court needs to review all of her financial documents, she has to admit that she's got, as Quang-ha says, "crazy mad money."

I'm not supposed to see any of this, but Pattie and Jairo didn't follow any of the correct procedures and that means that Lenore has to bring out the paperwork while I'm in the room.

Judge Biederman says that she is going to overlook all of the red tape for now.

I can see that Pattie likes the idea of red tape.

Obviously because of her attachment to the color.

I can't remember ever in my life seeing red tape. There is black and of course brown tape for packing. And silver.

I make a note to investigate this reference later.

Lenore signs off on her part in the approval process, but she says that Pattie and Jairo need to come back and do things the right way.

But the important thing is that for today, they are granted, jointly, the guardianship, which is on track to not be temporary, of a person named Willow Chance.

That's now legal.

Once this is said by the judge, in an official way, Dell makes a show by dropping to the floor like he's doing a split.

It's supposed to be some kind of victory move.

But he rips his pants in the crotch, which isn't just super-embarrassing for him but makes Quang-ha start to laugh.

It's his high-pitched giggle.

And once that happens, the contagious thing gets going.

And I'm part of that now.

I can see from the look on the judge's scrunched face that it's time for us to be moving on.

We are outside when Mai gives me a big hug.

Then Quang-ha slings his arm around my shoulder and I know he's going to say something important.

He lowers his voice, and I hear:

"I have a paper due in English class on Wednesday. *Moby-Dick*. Hope you have time to read it."

We then walk across the plaza and get into Jairo's taxi. We sit three in the front and three in the back.

It doesn't look safe, but there are seat belts for all of the passengers.

We decide to drive to Luigi's restaurant (since this is a favorite of Dell's and he's got the most enthusiasm about eating).

I get sacco beans, which are pinto beans marinated in oil and vinegar and crushed red pepper.

Everyone else orders spicy pickled tongue sandwiches.

I don't eat meat. And organ meat is in a whole other category of stuff I wouldn't want to chew.

But I do nothing but smile when they all offer me a bite.

chapter 61

W e are in the taxi, driving back, when Pattie reveals
something big.

She wants to buy the building.

The Gardens of Glenwood.

We all think that she's kidding, but apparently she has
already spoken to someone at the bank and she's put in
a formal offer.

I don't know what to make of it, but Dell looks thrilled.

I'm thinking that he's thinking that he won't get evicted
if she owns the place.

But I doubt he'd still be the building rep.

Quang-ha is the most energized by this news. I guess
he still worries about going back to the garage behind the
salon.

He says that if his mom owns the place, we should
make a skateboard ramp in the front entrance where the
stairs are.

I didn't know he was a skateboarder.

Interesting.

Pattie says that nothing is for certain.

That is the truest statement I've ever heard.

In the late afternoon, after everything has settled down, I put away my garden clothes and I run the mile loop.

I then take a seat next to the timber bamboo in the courtyard.

I know that I will think about this day many times.

Then I realize that it is the 7th of the month. And I'm not surprised.

7 is a natural number.

And it is a prime number.

There are 7 basic types of catastrophes.

And 7 days of the week.

Isaac Newton identified the 7 colors of the rainbow as:

Violet

Indigo

Blue

Green

Yellow

Orange

Red

Dell put people in 7 categories:

Misfit

Oddball

Lone Wolf

Weirdo

Genius

Dictator

Mutant

I have my own system of order.

I think that at every stage of living, there are 7 people who matter in your world.

They are people who are inside you.

They are people you rely on.

They are people who daily change your life.

For me I count:

1. My mom (always)

2. and my dad (forever)

3. Mai

4. Dell

5. Quang-ha

6. Pattie

7. Jairo

I decide that when my head begins to pound from now on, I will shut my eyes and count *to* 7, instead of *by* 7s.

I see each one of these people like the colors of the rainbow.

They are vivid and distinct.

And they hold a permanent place in my heart.

If the builder had had more money, this area would have probably been a swimming pool.

But it's not.

It's a garden.

I shift my position and suddenly I feel something in my pocket.

It's my lucky acorn.

I get up and pick a spot off to the side where I know there might be space for something of size to grow. I punch my finger into the dirt to make a small hole, and I drop in the brown nut.

I return to the stairs, and as I sit here in a slice of winter sunlight, two small birds find their way down to the honeysuckle planted next to the bamboo.

They speak to me, not in words, but in action.

They tell me that life goes on.

Acknowledgments

I would like to thank Jennifer Bailey Hunt and Lauri Hornik, who were my editors. They made this book. I tried to quit on multiple occasions. They wouldn't let me. I express my complete gratitude to both of you.

I had two agents in writing this book. Ken Wright and Amy Berkower. Everyone in the world should have the kind of support these two people give to writers.

I had many great teachers, but 7 who absolutely changed my life. Sharon Wetterling (Condon Elementary School, Eugene, Oregon), Harriet Wilson (South Eugene High School), Arnie Laferty (Roosevelt Middle School, Eugene, Oregon) Ray Scofield (Roosevelt Middle School), Wayne Thompson (Roosevelt Middle School), Dorothy Iz (Robert College in Istanbul, Turkey), and Addie Holsing (Willard Middle School, Berkeley, California). Thank you for giving so much of yourself to kids.

I have many writers who are my friends. More than

7. The writing pals (besides my husband) who personally inspire me daily are Evgenia Citkowitz. Maria Semple. Aaron Hartzler. Lucy Gray. Mart Crowley. Gayle Forman. Charlie Hauck. Henry Murray. Allan Burns. Nadine Schiff. Elaine Pope. Henry Louis Gates. Diane English. Nancy Meyers. Bill Rosen. Stephen Godchaux. Ry Cooder. David Thomson. Amy Holden Jones. And John Corey Whaley.

My mother, Robin Montgomery, is there for me in everything I attempt to do. And I thank her for all of her insight, wisdom, and humor. I was fortunate to have 7 other moms growing up, and so to my mother thank-you list I add Bertie Weiss, Ann Kleinsasser, Risha Meledandri, Jane Moshofsky, Donna Addison, Mary Rozaire, and Connie Herlihy.

I need to thank Thu Le and Minh Nguyen for helping me with the Vietnamese language.

And finally the 7 people who are present every day in so many ways. Farley Ziegler. Tim Goldberg. Randy Goldberg. Anne Herlihy. Max Sloan. Calvin Sloan.

And Gary Rosen.

Love you (7 letters).